VIOLET WINSPEAR

the girl at goldenhawk

HARLEQUIN BOOKS
toronto-winnipeg

SBN 373-70598-0
Harlequin Presents edition published June 1975

CHAPTER ONE

THE sea was so incredibly blue, as if rinsed out from
sapphires melted by that hot sun beating down on the white-
gold beach.

The slim and ringless hands of Jaine Dare gripped the
iron-grilled railing of the balcony upon which she stood.
Sozinha, as the Brazilian people called it, all on her own.
She took a deep breath of the hot, strange and pungent air,
perfumed by the sea and the coral and the lush flora that
grew in this part of the world.

The sun lay brazen upon the waves as they raced in over
the coral beds and unrolled like rich silk upon the sands.
The scene was both a delight and a pain in the eyes of the
English girl, who was more accustomed to the moderate
displays to be seen on the shores of her own land. Her gaze
ran over a bed of huge shiny boulders at the edge of the
beach, rising to a headland smothered in wild orchids and
feathery dwarf-palms, leading to a township called Porto de
Zanto.

The Port of Zanto had its place in history on account of
the nuns who were carried off from their convent by pirate
raiders and ransomed for rubies from the coffers of the
Duque Pedro Almanzor de Ros Zanto, lord of a million
acres of Brazilian territory, including this port and all the
surrounding countryside. Jaine had read about it in the
guide book she had bought at Rio airport; it had all seemed
rather romantic, especially when it stated that the Duque
Pedro of those days had loved one of the kidnapped nuns,
who had entered the convent of the Wailing Doves after
she and the Duque had quarrelled.

Suddenly there was a shimmer of tears in Jaine's eyes as
the painful delight of this place acted upon her usually con-

5

trolled emotions. From early childhood she had been dependent upon relatives for the reluctant affection usually eked out to an orphan, so it wasn't easy for Jaine to unlock her heart to people or places. She could never be certain of the welcome she would receive; she had learned that the world accepts the secure and rejects the insecure. And she had learned an even harder lesson, that the pretty are smiled upon more readily than the plain, and when the plain are poor the smiles are usually rare and perfunctory.

Dragging her gaze from the sands that shimmered in the sun, damascened as fine old armour, she rested her eyes on the palm trees sprouting gold and green from the land, their fronds like many points of emerald. How much she could like this place, if only she dared! But she came only for the wedding, and then with Madge, mother of the bride, she would return to England to take up as before as companion, secretary and go-between of the volatile and often impossible Madge Desmond, never a great actress but certainly a performer in the grand style.

That style of hers was much in evidence as Madge came sweeping into the room whose balcony doors were flung wide to frame the figure of Jaine at the iron-grilled rail. Jaine was her niece as well as her secretary and for this reason she was never too polite or considerate.

'If you're standing there mooning at some black-eyed Romeo, then I should forget it! Don't be taken in by the smouldering charm – these Brazilians aren't as romantic as they appear to be!'

Jaine swung round to look at Madge, whom she realized at once to be on the verge of an explosive row with someone. The painted blue eyes were like stones and her silk coat swished as she crossed to the balcony doors and stood there staring straight at Jaine. She might have been acting out a scene for a new play . . . one which Jaine sensed was highly charged with real emotions instead of theatrical ones.

Madge in a mood was someone to notice, fairly tall for a

6

woman, regal and silk-clad, with auburn hair that owed its style but not its colour to the skill of the hairdresser. As a girl she had been lovely, and so was her daughter, but Jaine bore no trace of the family looks. By contrast she was thin as a rake, with startling emerald eyes and raven hair cut short, rather like that of a page at the old Norman courts. Her cheekbones were detailed, like her eyebrows, and small shadows collected in the angles of her face. A producer friend of Madge's had once said of her that she was like a brownie, a pixy, with no apparent sex to her. It had been said in fun but meant in earnest, for none of Madge's stage friends had ever bothered to flirt with Jaine.

All at once Madge's full red lips drew into a thin scarlet line and her polished fingernails scraped the silk of her coat like a cat's claws. Jaine might have flinched, but she was curiously fearless, as the lonely and the unloved learn to be. She felt the mounting tension in every bone of her body, but showed no sign of it in that hotel bedroom above the ocean and the exotic scenery of a land she had never dreamed of seeing, not even when she heard the news that her cousin had become engaged to a Brazilian landowner. She waited in patient silence for the explosive words to flicker and flash from Madge's lips, though for the life of her she couldn't think what might have occurred to touch off the French–Irish temper that she shared with the Desmonds but which she had learned to control by reason of her debt of gratitude. Madge had given her a home all those years ago, paid for her education, and employed her, and Jaine, in a world of lessening loyalties, was grateful not to have been put into an institution where charity was clad in a uniform.

'Jaine,' the storm was gathering, 'do come in from there and stop draping yourself over that balcony like Juliet! I've something to tell you and I don't want the entire hotel to overhear me.'

The warm and sensual voice, so beloved of London

theatregoers, was charged with a bitter fury, and Jaine entered the room at once and closed the balcony doors behind her. 'What on earth is the matter, Madge?' She never used the term 'aunt', having been ordered long ago not to do so. As an actress Madge had a fetish about age and she considered that the term was ageing.

With a gesture of impatient anger Madge flung off her silk coat and reached into her handbag for her cigarette-case. Her fingernails shone silver against silver as she extracted one of the expensive cigarettes and waited for Jaine to apply the lighter that stood on the sofa table. As smoke issued from her taut nostrils and she flung back her head in a gesture of arrogance, Jaine was reminded of the many times she had seen Madge Desmond act out a dramatic scene from a stage play. But this time the curtain was down, the theatre lights were out, and the scene was real.

Something was wrong, and Jaine tensed like a young emerald-eyed cat who senses danger and is uncertain if it will affect her.

'There isn't going to be a wedding!' Madge said it with shocking distinctness and flung ash off her cigarette to the carpeted floor. 'Your cousin Laraine is not going to marry the Duque!'

Of all the things Jaine had expected to hear this was the very least of them. It was a bombshell, bursting in that hotel room and reverberating in Jaine's ears. She sank down on the edge of the long sofa and stared at Madge ... the news was incredible in the face of what she knew about Laraine's determined ambition to land a husband who was not only titled and rich, but who was still on the sunny side of forty.

'It's probably only a tiff—' she began. 'Pre-wedding nerves and all that – it will blow over.'

'Over my dead body!' Madge cut the air with these devastating words. 'Laraine, even if I do say it and shouldn't, being her mother, is one of the loveliest and most eligible

8

girls in England. Her father left her well provided for, even if I admit that her attractive fortune bears little resemblance to the wealth of the Duque. She could marry any one of a number of eligible young men, and when she chose to pursue this Brazilian I said nothing beyond that I thought it a pity that he had a son already and this son would inherit his title. But you know Laraine when she sets her mind to something – or someone. She was insistent that she and this man would be ideally suited and she persuaded me to agree to the marriage. I even listened to her argument that a quiet and simple wedding would be preferable to a showy one, as I thought at the time that the Duque had been married before and would prefer a simple affair. Now, of all things, I am told that the man has never been married before – that his child is the result of a romance he once had, and that his object in marrying at all is to provide this boy Tristao with a mother young and pretty enough to appeal to him. Furthermore, the boy is a lame youngster, having suffered an injury in a car accident when he was three years old.'

At that point Madge broke off dramatically and stubbed out her cigarette with angry movements of her hand. 'The boy can't help his disability, of course. And if the Duque has been a philanderer, then one can only be as tolerant as possible about it. But for him to presume that he is going to shut my Laraine up in his *fortaleza*, away from all the fun of life, the bright lights and gaiety she loves so much, just to be a mother-figure to his – his love child, then he is sadly mistaken. I have told Laraine that she doesn't have to go through with such an arrangement, but the poor darling seems afraid of the man. She says he has a fearful Latin temper and she just won't tell him to his face that she can't go through with the marriage.'

Jaine had listened to all this in stunned amazement. She had presumed herself that the Duque was a widower, and to hear that he was openly the proud father of a son born out of wedlock struck Jaine as being the very height of soph-

9

istication – especially for a Latin, when one heard so much about the chastity of Latin women and the sacred regard their men had for them.

'Laraine must have suspected he had a fiery temper before becoming engaged to him,' Jaine murmured. 'It would be a foregone conclusion that a Brazilian landowner was unlikely to be tame and manageable. Is Laraine quite certain that she's out of love with him?'

Madge gave her niece what could only be termed a look of worldly disdain. 'You read too many romantic novels,' she said crisply. 'We are talking of marriage, an agreeable and workable alliance between two people who wish to be husband and wife and not master and slave. I told Laraine from the very beginning that a Latin bridegroom was bound to take a more arrogant view of marriage than a pleasant and easygoing Englishman. I warned her, and being headstrong she chose to ignore my warning. Now this has happened! She finds the situation unbearable and I, as her mother, am expected to extract her from the contretemps with the minimum of fuss and no bother.'

The actress let forth her most dramatic sigh and flung out her jewelled wrists as if in supplication to the gods. 'As I see it, Jaine, with regard to the man involved, it's asking for the moon to expect him to release Laraine from the engagement without fireworks. To these people an engagement is a serious business, almost as binding as a marriage service, and I truly believe that I'm going to have to smuggle Laraine out of Brazil before the Duque gets wind that the wedding is off.'

Jaine had heard some brazen things from Madge in her time, but this suggestion beat the lot. 'You can't do that!' she exclaimed. 'It's only good manners to tell him to his face – after all, he is a titled person and of importance here in Brazil. Laraine can't treat him as casually as she treated the Honourable Billy Hopgood.'

'I quite agree that she treated Billy unfairly, and when we

get back to England I'm going to persuade her to give him another chance. He's rather a nice boy – manageable and agreeable, and there is a chance of the title if that flying brother of his ever crashes his plane.' Madge placed her fingers at her temples, and her blue eyes dwelt with almost hypnotic intensity upon Jaine. 'I've been good to you, haven't I?'

The words came suddenly, cool and incised as the diamonds glittering on Madge's arms.

Jaine sat as still and straight as a figure struck in marble. Her dark hair had a silken stillness about her head, and there was not a quiver to her lips. Her eyes were so green they might have been jewels set in her fine-boned, unpainted young face. Her eyebrows were wings of stillness above her eyes, poised in flight now the message had been carried into Jaine's startled mind.

'Yes,' she said quietly. 'You've been good to me.'

'And Laraine has treated you almost like a sister?'

'Almost,' Jaine agreed.

'Then do you see what I'm getting at?'

'Not quite,' said Jaine, for it seemed too incredible to believe, that she was being asked to act as go-between, dogsbody, bringer of the direful news that the lovely Laraine now declined to go through with her marriage to the present Duque Pedro Almanzor de Ros Zanto.

'No!' Jaine leapt to her feet and her green eyes came alive with rebellion. 'I won't do it, Madge! It isn't fair of you to ask such a thing of me! To play on my sense of duty – loyalty – call it what you will. I'm grateful for being given a home and a job, but I'm not begging for a clip round the jaw from Laraine's outraged fiancé. Let her face her own music!'

'Darling.' In an instant Madge became the very essence of charm and beguilement. She came to her niece and took firm hold of her thin young hands, pressing the fine bones with her rings. 'You really are the only person who can look as innocent as a babe when you deliver – and I admit it – outrageous messages from me. You are so clear-eyed and obviously virgin that no man dreams ⌐f taking offence. The Duque will not be the exception to that rule, very well proved in the four years you've worked for me. Jaine, you are the perfect answer to Laraine's prayer, and you are fond of her, aren't you? She is the nearest person you have for a sister, and I'm sure you wouldn't want to see her forced into a marriage with a man she doesn't truly care for. Now would you?'

'It seems to me,' said Jaine, who had to be practical in the face of all this emotion, 'a pity that Laraine didn't make sure of her feelings before she accepted the Duque's proposal of marriage. It also seems to me, in view of his Don Juan tendencies, a mark in Laraine's favour that he went as far as to ask her to be his wife. Just think, Madge, if she goes ahead and marries him the title of *duquesa* will be hers. What more could she wish?'

'Are you being funny?' The blue eyes of Madge Desmond bored into Jaine like a pair of gimlets. 'Be careful, my pet. You have no family apart from Laraine and myself, and the world can be a big empty place to someone homeless, and without the weapons for hooking a man. It isn't only that you're plain-looking, Jaine. You have a curious sexless quality ... like a cartoon cat, or a pierrot perched in the hook of the moon. You've grown accustomed to the life I live. You enjoy the theatre and I can take it all away from you in the winking of an eyelid. Poor child, you'd be an actress yourself if you had the looks – now wouldn't you? Well, I'm offering you the chance to act for Laraine and myself, and if you've any gratitude to offer me for all I've done for you, then you'll do this little thing – won't you?'

The beguilement had evaporated like smoke in the air and in its place was the insolent panache and daring which had won for Madge Desmond a position in the theatre which could not be snatched from her in the winking of an eyelid.

Despite an instant flare of anger that anyone should say such things, even to her, Jaine also felt a reluctant amusement and a touch of the admiration she usually felt for one of Madge's more inspired performances. Madge was a fighter, and right now, in her own unscrupulous way, she was fighting for her spoiled and only child. Madge knew that a personal confrontation with Duque Pedro would result only in a clash of strong wills and wounding language ... but Jaine was someone whom men either dismissed as a youthful nonentity, or found disconcerting for the unflawed candour of her huge green eyes.

One glance at Jaine was sufficient to inform most men that she was uncorrupted by them, by life, by fortune and misfortune. She was, in fact, one of those rare people whose eyes were truly the windows of her compassionate soul. She liked neither to hurt nor to be hurt, but had found all the same that she often did get hurt.

Right now Madge was physically hurting her fingers by gripping them so that her big-stoned rings dug into Jaine's bones.

'See the Duque for Laraine, and for me, and you won't lose out on the deal,' Madge urged. 'It's about time you had a fur coat, and when we get back to London I'll take you to my own fur man and we'll pick you out something really nice, to cuddle up against that funny, big-eyed face of yours.'

'I – I don't want to be bribed.' Jaine tore free of Madge's hands and turned to gaze from the balcony doors, which were of glass, so the Brazilian sunlight streamed into the room. Life was a curious affair. She would have loved to stay in this exotic country for a while, yet Laraine, who had the chance to live here, was throwing it all up on the flimsy basis that a man was marrying her to provide a mother for his son. Jaine, who was totally uncorrupted, was not offended by the child's illegitimacy. The boy couldn't help the man that his father was, and in a way the Duque was

13

trying to make up for past mistakes by marrying someone young and pretty for the boy to accept and grow to love...

Jaine swung again to face Madge and her eyes were sheerest emerald as they caught the sunlight. 'Is Laraine quite certain that she can't – or won't go through with the marriage? She isn't just having a tantrum, which she'll regret later on? This man probably has quite a lot of Latin pride, and once he's told...'

'You'll do it?' Madge broke in... so eagerly that it struck Jaine that her aunt was possibly as scared of the Duque's temper as Laraine was. An amazing thing, for Jaine had seen Madge reduce sister actresses to tears, and make mincemeat of the ideas and orders of playwrights and producers.

Curiosity stirred through Jaine Dare. She had not as yet met the ducal fiancé of her cousin, and she began to form a mental picture of a fierce-eyed roué, who ate lovely blonde girls for breakfast, and could probably make hash of a plain and virtuous secretary who dared to tell him that his engagement was off and his fiancée was in transit to the safe and moderate shores of England.

'Is he very terrible?' The words had to be asked, though Jaine held out no hope that Madge would be strictly truthful with her. 'I gather it was the title that attracted Laraine? After all, if she had fallen in love with the man she wouldn't be giving up this easily.'

'Love is a lot of nonsense,' Madge said flatly. 'It's for *au pair* girls and typists; the bit of sugar to sweeten that two-up, two-down on a lifelong mortgage. Laraine doesn't have to worry about such foolishness, and if I had felt she could make an agreeable set-up of this marriage, then I would have persuaded her to go through with it. But it has to be faced that Latin men restrict their wives to the home, even if they themselves enjoy a good time. It would be a high price for Laraine to pay, and she can find herself an equally well-off husband back home, who will allow her her little privileges.'

'What, romantic affairs on the side?' Jaine just had to ask.

'Laraine is lovely,' Madge's blue eyes swept up and down the very slim figure of her niece, clad in a plain green skirt and a pintucked white shirt. 'Men have always noticed her and made a lot of her. Why should such an adornment to society be tucked away in one man's house – like a museum piece? No! I won't see her forced into the wrong kind of marriage. I'd be a poor sort of mother if I did that. Poor darling Laraine! She's shaking in her shoes that the Duque will do something drastic if she sees him again, so my plan is that she and I fly out of Brazil this very evening, while you, Jaine, arrange a meeting with him and in your very best puritan style explain the situation. He can only rant at you—'

Madge shrugged her elegant shoulders. 'Well, you won't mind that, will you? It's all in a good cause, and just think what Jeanne d'Arc went through!'

Jaine could only gaze at Madge and be amazed by her sheer impudence and bold determination. First she had bullied and now she challenged Jaine to live up to her surname. Dare the Duque, if she dared! But this wasn't a game, and the old days were over, when Laraine would dare her to leap steps or jump in at the deep end of the school pool.

'Laraine will never truly grow up,' she told Madge, 'while you allow her to play with people's lives and emotions. People aren't her toys, you know.'

Madge merely smiled. 'Don't be such a little evangelist, my pet. It's what puts off the men in your case . . . they see too much virtue in you and not enough vamp. Anyway, it won't break the Duque's heart to learn that Laraine has had second thoughts about marrying him; a man with his kind of reputation is hardly likely to be sentimental. He'll let fly with his Latin temper, and it's better that he let fly at you,

Jaine, rather than at me. Those big, cool green eyes of yours will soon quench his fury, but I'm too likely to let him know what I think of a man who romances Laraine and then arrogantly informs her that his main object in settling down is to provide a mother for his lame young son, who I understand has been legalized as the Duque's heir. He even went as far as to tell my Laraine that the boy Tristao has first call on his affections, and he felt he should make this clear to her. He then put an expensive bracelet on her wrist, stated that his lawyers would draw up settlement papers, and quite hypnotized her until she returned to the hotel last night and realized all at once that she would suffocate, or go crazy, shut up in a Latin household with an invalid child, her life ordered and commanded by a Latin aristocrat who obviously has no intention of changing his own way of life.

'Laraine begged me to do something,' said Madge, dramatically, 'and I felt sure, Jaine, that you would be only too willing to help out. You have a certain gallantry – that little bit of nerve that makes it possible for you to face up to things that put pretty, gay, clothes-conscious girls like Laraine into a flap. You're a born go-between, a treasure in your way, and I shan't be ungrateful, Jaine.'

'I'm not asking for a reward.' Jaine gave her aunt a straight look. 'I'm agreeing to see the Duque because there is every chance that he has told his son about Laraine, and someone owes it to him to be frank and above board. If I refuse to confront him with the news, then he'll be left to learn about it from the newspapers when you and Laraine arrive back in London. That sort of let-down would make him really furious, and I can tell, Madge, that you've made up your mind not to see him.'

'Well,' Madge turned aside from Jaine's accusing eyes and gathered up her silk coat, 'I don't fancy the attendant fuss and bother. Latin people aren't like us. They make such a song and dance about these things, as if marriage was still some sort of holy institution. From now on I'll see to it that

16

Laraine flirts only with English or American boys. I'll stand for no more mix-ups with hot-tempered Latins. She's far too pretty and volatile to be able to stand their intensity, for it's a foregone conclusion that the Duque Pedro has it in mind to provide a clutch of brothers and sisters for his adored love-child.'

With a rustle of silk Madge made for the door. There she paused and flung an inquiring look at Jaine. 'You won't change your mind about seeing him?'

Jaine shook her head.

'Don't make things too bad for Laraine. Tell him that she felt she would be too homesick for England – something like that.'

Jaine made no answer to this, standing as tense as a foil in the hand of fate as Madge closed the door behind her and left her niece alone with her troubled thoughts.

Dare the Duque . . . whose name of Pedro stood for stone . . . for cruel.

CHAPTER TWO

WITHOUT much difficulty Jaine managed to hire a car with the aid of the hotel receptionist, though the young man's polite smile slipped a little when she told him that she wished to be taken to the Casa de Rocha – the house of the rocks, as the coastal home of the Duque was called.

The man at the wheel drove expertly and silently along a twisting road that gave dazzling glimpses of the sea, and of tiny fishing hamlets tucked beneath the towering, almost sinister cliffs, edged by shrubs that hung a display of colourful foliage down over the rocks. She saw beaches where peak-hulled fishing boats were drawn up on the sands, their coloured sails furled now the morning catch had been carried to the harbour sheds.

It all added up to a picture that distracted her for the time being, the clusters of small painted houses on the cliff slopes, with drop balconies of pierced woodwork, set amid small plantations of shaggy green banana trees, tall sugar-canes, and waving heads of maize.

A vivid and primitive scenery, coming alive out of canvases painted a century ago and never altered by a single antique tile or splash of waves on worn old walls. Despite her nervous desire to have her errand over and done with as quickly as possible, Jaine couldn't help but respond to all that she saw on her way to the Duque. She had been out of England before, but Madge Desmond was essentially a Paris and New York person and this was the first time she had brought Jaine to a place such as Porto de Zanto, which was unspoiled by the so-called march of progress. Here there were no towering blocks of glass and concrete, no ear-splitting duel of traffic horns, and none of that choked feeling of breathing air poisoned by the fumes of petrol and polluted

18

riverbeds.

In through the open car windows stole the pungency of the wide ocean, and the rich earthy scents wafted from the plantations of fruit and coffee: sugar and maize.

Jaine's eyes followed the swooping wings of a pinky-fawn bird as it flew from the cliffside as the car sped by. Up and up, free to make its nest in this wonderful place, where apart from the hoopoes the big eagles dwelt on the high crests of the Brazilian mountains. Jaine felt herself captivated by this place, her enchanted gaze falling again to the fishing boats adorned by a pattern of diamonds or an immense lashed eye; boats protected by the sun-god, a pagan and exciting superstition not out of place in this land of the sun.

How marvellous to be so free, for despite her lack of parental ties Jaine felt tied by a sense of duty to those who had taken her in, and fed and clothed her until she was grown up and qualified to earn her living as Madge's very efficient secretary. She had vocally and silently rebelled against the duty she was performing today for Madge, but all the same she was going through with it. A 'poor relation' as she undoubtedly was had instilled into her from an early age the knife-edge, the prod of being duty-bound to pay back whenever possible some part of the debt in being a poor relation who had cost time, money and care to those who had not been compelled to rear an orphan.

A small, ironical smile touched Jaine's lips. Her irresponsible cousin Laraine had a little money of her own, and so she was entitled to be called a woman of independence. But Jaine, who had an inborn sense of responsibility, must always think of herself as an orphan, a dependant, a person faced by a cool and hostile world if she chose not to pick up the pieces of Laraine's broken dolls, and broken romances.

Oh, she knew well enough that she could have walked out on Madge and gone elsewhere for a secretarial position, but that prod of loyalty, that rather amused affection held her back. While she stayed with Madge she had some colour in her life; some drama and a few crumbs of gaiety. If she left, then the confines of a bedsitter would close around her, enlivened only by a nine-to-five-thirty job in the city. She would miss the Desmond tirades, the rehearsals for new plays, the coming and going at Madge's Westminster flat of stage celebrities, TV personalities, journalists and writers.

None of them ever really noticed her, but Jaine was a born spectator and she enjoyed watching the by-play of life from the wings of Madge's household.

It was all she really had, and to hold on to it she took this drive to the Casa de Rocha, and nerved herself to tell the Duque Pedro that last night his fiancée had left for London with her mother, her engagement to him broken. In Jaine's handbag was the jewel-box containing the betrothal bracelet of diamonds, the earclips to match, and the solitaire pendant. Even Madge had been a trifle shocked when Laraine had said airily that she felt like keeping the jewellery. After all, the Duque was incredibly well off and he wouldn't begrudge her the diamonds – mined from his own land in the north, cut by an expert, and designed for only one purpose, to adorn a pretty woman.

'You will most certainly give back the diamonds,' Madge had said, in quite a sharp tone of voice. 'If you are going to make the break from Pedro de Zanto, then you will make it a clean one. He isn't an easy-going Englishman who might shrug off the matter of an ex-fiancée holding on to a gift of jewellery. He's an unpredictable Latin, and we don't know yet how he'll react to the news which Jaine is going to break to him.'

Jaine, feeling the oblong shape of the jewel-box in her suede handbag, felt her throat go dry at the same time. The hired car had made a turn into a driveway between immense stone gateposts; a drive lined with giant tropical trees of great width and stature, with almost a blue tinge to their majestic trunks. Their huge crests met above the drive and formed a tunnel of cool blue-green shadow, so that Jaine had an impression of being suddenly cut off from the vivid sea landscape and driven into the nave of some great forest.

On and on swept the car, going deeper into the heart of the Duque's estate, the beaches and the boats and the glimpses she had had of brown-skinned fisherfolk left behind.

Suddenly, fiercely, she wished that she had stood out against Madge and refused to undertake such a danger-tinged mission. What did she know of Pedro de Zanto? Laraine had been so obviously scared to face him herself that it seemed beyond doubt that he had a terrible temper ... and out of a sense of dutiful affection Jaine was putting her own head on the block.

What an absurd little idiot she was! She half leaned forward as if to tap on the glass partition separating her from the driver of the car; the impulse to curtail this visit before it began was all she was aware of a second before the drive-way opened out into a large courtyard and she caught her first glimpse of the Casa de Rocha, and saw the cobbled walls that gave the house its name.

Jaine was startled ... almost disappointed, for she had ex-pected a certain grandeur and was confronted by a strange, almost grim habitation.

A *fortaleza* Madge had called it, and indeed the large *casa* did have the appearance of being built to keep out strangers and to contain within its high rock-like walls the private loves and hates of the Zanto family, which was such an old one that its history went far back in the annals of Portuguese discovery of Brazil, when the titled captains used to set out in their full-sailed galleons in search of new worlds, whose resources were instantly plundered to provide wealth for the motherland ... Portugal of the Golden Age.

Jaine must have tapped the glass partition without being aware, for it suddenly slid back and the driver, who spoke a smattering of English, turned to ask Jaine what she required.

'Oh – are you sure this is the home of the Duque?' she asked.

'This is the Casa de Rocha,' he replied. 'The *excellentissimo senhor* has other houses, of course, in other parts of Brazil. To this one he comes when he has business concerning the sugar fields, but it is well known that his preferred home is that where his coffee lands are situated. A great house, *senhorita*. Beautiful as this one is not. And called Goldenhawk, which was the name of the vessel in which the Duque's most illustrious ancestor first sailed into the waters of southern America. In fact the name Goldenhawk was applied to the master as well as the ship – if you understand me?'

Yes, Jaine understood him immediately. She could well understand such an appellation bèing applied to a tawny-skinned, plundering hawk of a Portuguese duke, set on finding treasure in the new world, and of lining his own nest with golden nuggets.

She turned to look again at the house of rocks, which might well be built on the site of the first establishment built by the Goldenhawk; a sort of fortress against the Indians who would have dwelt among those fantastic tropical trees; a forest in those days, which the Duque had speedily tamed and turned into a plantation.

She was more than ever hesitant about entering the Casa de Rocha, but in that moment the driver of the car left his seat and opened the door beside her. She realized that she would look a fool if, having come all this way, she now told the driver to take her back to the hotel. Nerving herself, she slid from the car and told the man to wait for her. She went up the steps of the Casa to the formidable carved door, beside which hung one of those old-fashioned bells that had to be pulled, and which set up a sonorous clamour beyond the panels of the front door. Jaine's fingers clenched her handbag . . . this was it! When that door opened she would learn whether the Duque was at home, and whether or not he would see her. In the event that she was told he was too occupied to see her, then she had a letter in her handbag written by Madge. Not a letter of explanation, but one which requested the Duque to spare her secretary a few minutes of his time.

The door opened at last, with a kind of lordly deliberation. A manservant confronted her, clad in a dark livery that emphasized the stern politeness of his swarthy face. Jaine swallowed the dryness from her throat and suddenly decided that only Madge's letter would gain admittance for her. She took the envelope from her bag. 'I am here on the behalf of Mrs. Desmond,' she explained. 'Would you please show this to His Excellency and request that I see him. It is rather – important.'

She had taken it for granted that the manservant would understand her, but he seemed to look at her with a kind of stony displeasure. Then he accepted the letter, glanced at the heading, and then beckoned her into the hall of the Casa.

Left to wait while the letter was carried to the Duque, Jaine noticed that the floor of the hall was of inlaid wood with an ancient sheen to it. There were pointed windows set high around the hall and the colours of wild sunsets seemed to mingle their colours in the painted glass. It was as if the builder of the house had been thinking of a Portuguese chapel, for the slanting coloured light across the floor gave that impression, as did the dark carved furniture, and the sombre gleam of silver lamps and silverware upon a great side table.

Then all at once Jaine caught her own reflection in a wall mirror in a darkly carved frame, and she felt a sudden sense of unreality as her own face stared back at her, the emerald of her eyes brilliant against the pallor of her skin. She looked afraid and was annoyed by this; she didn't want to appear frightened of her mission and of the Duque, and she braced her spine, tilted her chin, and turned her gaze away from that disheartening mirror. If only she had some part of Laraine's attraction; those big distractingly blue eyes, that plume of red-gold hair, those lips that were so seductively pink and full. It had come as no surprise to Jaine that her cousin had induced a rich Latin to fall for her charms ... but now that she saw the Casa de Rocha she understood a little why the spoiled and pleasure-loving Laraine had fled the master and couldn't tell him to his face that she no longer fancied being his wife.

If the Duque Pedro Almanzor de Ros Zanto was as grim and stony as this place, then Laraine had Jaine's sympathy if not her gratitude for landing her with the task of telling the Duque he had been jilted.

She tensed as footsteps approached from the direction of the stairs, which the manservant had mounted with the letter in his hand. He returned without it and said in stilted English that she was to follow him. The Senhor Duque would spare her a few minutes of his time.

The Senhor Duque was gracious, she thought, but as she mounted the stairs in the wake of his manservant her legs had a tremor in them and she wasn't feeling half as courageous as her thoughts. They went along a tiled corridor a little less sombre than the hall, the reason being the balconies at either end of it, letting sunlight over the ironwork and into the house. The manservant paused in front of a pair of doors, then he took hold of the carved handles and opened the doors with an impressive sweep of his arms. He stood aside for Jaine to enter the rather formal room, which she took to be the *sala da visita*, for all the furniture was dignified and there was not a cushioned seat in sight.

She stepped into the room and at once the doors closed behind her. She glanced around as if expecting to see the Duque, but the room was empty but for its furniture and the great square carpet on the tiled floor. She stood there in the centre of the carpet and felt as if someone were deliberately playing on her already unsettled nerves. It was like waiting for the dentist! If one were shown instantly into the presence of the tormentor, then what courage one had hoarded had little chance to slip right away. But Jaine felt that her courage was almost at its last ebb as in the silence she listened to the only sound, that of a clock ticking in a glass case. She noticed that it had taken her about two hours to reach the Casa, that she had already waited some fifteen minutes for the Duque to present himself, and could reckon upon it being dark by the time she arrived back at the hotel. She would just have time for a quick meal before catching her local aeroplane to Rio in time to board the midnight jet bound for London, a journey in itself of just over eleven hours.

So much to do in so short a time . . . so little left of Porto de Zanto to see before she bade good-bye to its exotic scenery and its warm, blue and gold climate.

She sighed . . . and then felt her heart turn a somersault as those double doors suddenly swept open again. Their dark panels framed one of the tallest men she had ever seen, lithe and erect, wearing kneeboots of gleaming leather moulded to the strong calves of his legs. Tan breeches were belted into a flat, athletic waist, and a fine white linen shirt covered a broad chest and a pair of wide shoulders. The neck of the shirt was open against a tawny-skinned throat, and as Jaine's gaze rose to the man's face she knew instantly why Laraine had been fascinated and then terrified by this man.

Her cousin had thought she could enslave him and bend him to *her* caprices, and then had discovered that he placed no woman upon a pedestal but made of each one a captive of his dominating personality. The woman whom he married – for whatever reason – would be his total possession and subject to *his* will. Never would she be allowed to run almost free on the end of a long and tolerant leash.

Just in time Laraine had realized this . . . but Jaine, the onlooker and not the participant in romantic affairs, knew the kind of man he was the moment she set eyes on his face. Compelling and magnetic were overdone expressions, but in his case they applied in full. His eyes were as tawny as sherry, but the lines beside them were as incised as if shaped by steel on stone. There was nobility in his brow and in the strong facial bones ... it was strange that she should think this distinguished and striking man capable of diabolic behaviour ... yet that impression struck her at once.

From his black brows to his gleaming boots he was dangerous, and she, a loveless, lonely fool in dread of losing what little she had of Madge's affection, had entered his house in order to tell him that a woman, her cousin, had changed her mind about becoming his wife.

The double doors clicked to behind him and he came towards Jaine, holding her gaze with his. 'And what is it, *senhorita*, that you have come all this way to tell me? And why on earth do you look as if you might faint before getting out the words?'

Getting out even a single word did seem beyond Jaine, though it wasn't quite true that she felt faint. She felt extremely frightened. He was so tall, so boundlessly male, so foreign, and so much the lord of all this structure of carved stone and the land surrounding it. She had said flippantly to Madge that he might strike her for her presumption in coming here to say things Laraine should have said. But she hadn't really believed it possible ... until this moment, when she stood in the *sala da visita* of his house and found herself at the mercy of his eyes.

They held neither Latin fire nor Latin welcome. Across the room she had thought his eyes as tawny as sherry, but now they seemed to glitter and gleam like those of a puma on the prowl. Deliberately, arrogantly, with even a touch of insolence, he walked all round Jaine and took her in at every angle.

'Mrs. Desmond mentions in her letter that you are her niece as well as her secretary. You bear no resemblance to

26

her, or to her daughter. There is no auburn in your hair, no tinge of rose in your skin . . . your eyes are like jade absinthe, the wine of forgetfulness.'

Jaine could only stare at him with those eyes, and feel the wild hammering of her heart. He was wicked and strange, she thought. He had devastated Laraine with his attraction, and then sent her flying out of Brazil with all the speed that a jet plane could muster. Jaine wished wildly that she was beautiful so that she might insult him and tell him that his eyes were enough to break the wings of an angel!

'Well,' he said, 'are you going to deliver your message by word of mouth, or send it by way of thought transmission – which should not be too difficult for a green-eyed witch.'

'Really!' The word broke from Jaine's lips. 'You are a most arrogant man!'

'And is that the message you came to deliver from your aunt?' One of those night-black brows rose in sardonic inquiry.

Jaine just looked at him with a catch of her breath, for in a way he had hit upon the truth . . . it was his arrogance from which her cousin had fled. From the fascination which his figure and his face generated . . . until a woman realized that an iron will lay behind his tawny glance, and that the lithe masculine grace of his Latin body was a trap for the unwary female who thought she could take him.

All her life Laraine had enjoyed her own way, and since growing up she had become one of the most sought-after girls in London. For a time she had flirted with, and been pursued by the Honourable Billy Hopgood, until while on holiday in Portugal her path had crossed that of the Duque Pedro Almanzor de Ros Zanto, himself in the home country on a visit to relatives. Laraine had heard that Latin men were ardent lovers . . . and learned, in time, that those who proposed marriage, especially if they belonged to the titled classes, did not do so from a wildly romantic purpose but for reasons unclouded by the haze of adorning desire. They were

reared in the tradition of the arranged marriage, or the marriage of expediency, and it had been quite a blow to Laraine's vanity when she had found out that the Duque
required not so much a beautiful wife to adorn his place in
Latin society as a young and pretty mother for his son.

Laraine was very like her mother in one important respect,
she wanted to stay young for as long as possible, and the
sudden acquirement of a six-year-old son would overnight
have made her appear, in her own eyes at least, almost
matronly.

'And so, *senhorita*, out of the blue you arrive, a stranger to
me, to underline a facet of my doubtless unsaintly nature,
from which I am to assume . . . well, you tell me, and in the
process do sit down in a chair before I am compelled to
scoop you off the carpet. What is it? Are you shaking with
nerves, or have you not eaten a proper meal all day? Never
have I seen a face so devoid of colour – apart from the eyes –
and bones that so shape themselves to the eye of the be-
holder. Does Mrs. Desmond keep you locked away from the
sunlight, and does she throw you only scraps from her table?
What are you, for you don't seem of her world! Or of any
world unassociated with the fey or that connected with
wands and strange enchantments.'

Jaine instantly felt that she had stood just about enough
from this man, with his masterful stance, his mocking
regard, and distinctly wicked features. That banked-down
temper, inherited from her Huguenot ancestors who had fled
from the Inquisition to become silk-weavers in Ireland, suddenly flared alight in Jaine, and into his face she flung the
words that had been trembling on her lips all day, ever since
waking alone in her hotel room, her mind filled with the task
which Madge had left her to deal with.

'I'm the poor relation, *senhor*. The prideless creature who
grew up picking up after Laraine. Story books flung and
crumpled, dolls with cracked faces, scattered beads, and
broken crayons. But it didn't stop there, and I am once again

tidying up after my glamorous cousin.' With these words Jaine opened her handbag and reached inside for the red-leather jewel-box. She held it out to the Duque. 'Laraine has returned these to you, *senhor.* She has found herself unable to go through with her engagement to you, and I am asked to tell you that she is sorry but would have found herself home-sick for England as the bride of a man too well settled in Brazil to ever live anywhere else. Please take the jewellery. It's all there.'

His tawny glance dropped from her white – and if she did but know it – tormented face and dwelt on the red, velvet-lined box in which lay the glittering diamonds he had pre-sented to his prospective bride. His ducal crest was on the lid of the box, and it seemed certain to Jaine that he would resent most of all the fact that a woman had walked out on the title he had offered her.

'Would you please to put it on that table.' He gestured at a marble-topped table that stood nearby and in silence Jaine obeyed his order and was secretly glad to let go of the small fortune in gems which Madge had entrusted to her.

'I'm sorry—' she began, 'that Laraine lacked the courage to tell you herself that—'

'You, most obviously, are far braver!' His words had a fine cutting edge to them. 'Or is it the bravado of someone threatened with her livelihood unless she tidies up after the rich relations?'

The pallor of Jaine's cheeks was replaced by two flames that flickered over her cheekbones and shot sparks into her eyes. 'I'm not proud of my errand, *senhor,* but someone had to run it. It wouldn't have been fair if Laraine and my aunt had left you to learn about her departure in the newspapers. I know that Madge will already have spoken to the reporters back home – any sort of publicity is good for an actress if it gets her name into the papers.'

'Quite.' The word flickered like the tip of a lash. 'And so you came to break the news, and are you afraid that you

29

have broken my heart as well?'

'No—' Jaine looked at him as if she very much doubted the presence of a heart within that hard, tawny frame of his. 'I think the main reason Laraine ran away was that she felt you wanted her for convenience' sake rather than your own sake.' Jaine shrugged. 'I am sure you know what I mean.'

'Do I, *senhorita*?' The full devastation of his glance was directed upon her, so that she saw just how tawny were his eyes, just how black his lashes and brows. 'You mean that my passions were not as involved as they should have been and that I had my son's desires more strongly in mind than my own? And why not, when Tristao has been part of my life for six years, and the Senhorita Laraine has only skimmed the surface of it, like a pretty butterfly, snuffing honey and unprepared to share it with a small boy who cannot run and play as other boys.'

Abruptly the Duque snapped his fingers and his face became a chiselled mask. 'To the devil with your cousin! She is like too many other women who want to have their cake and to eat it, regardless of those condemned to the crumbs of life. I am surprised she sent back the diamonds. I wondered whether she would!'

Jaine stared at him when he said these words, and after a moment she saw a faintly sinister smile at the edge of his mouth. 'You look at me with a big question in your eyes, *senhorita*. Do you take me for a fool that I would not test a woman before taking her to the altar?'

'And you tested Laraine,' Jaine said quietly, 'by letting her know that you were marrying her for the sake of your son. You felt, I suppose, that if she had a compassionate heart she would love your son. I'm sorry you have been let down so badly.'

'The question of being let down has not yet arisen,' he said, and even as Jaine puzzled this over in her mind he pressed a bell beside the alcove of potted plants that replaced a fireplace in this very Latin room. 'You have had a long car ride and a long explanation to put forward, and now it is time for your thirst to be quenched. Will you prefer tea or coffee? We grow both in Brazil, of equal excellence. Tell me, do you find that you like Brazil?'

'I've not seen a lot of your country, *senhor*, but it seems a most colourful place.'

'Very unlike England, of course?'

'It couldn't be more unlike,' she agreed, and then fell silent, watching him under the dark lashes of her green eyes as a manservant entered the *sala* and he ordered refreshments. Tea as well as coffee, and a plate of cakes. Jaine's teeth caught at her underlip as she recalled his remark about her bones; he evidently thought she was half-starved, for she had no rich hint of curves, and none of that sensuous quality of the woman who is basically self-indulgent. As she was related to the Desmonds he had expected her to be like them, and she felt a faint twinge of amusement that she was so entirely unlike her aunt and her cousin.

She felt him looking her over with those strange and deeply brilliant eyes and all at once she became terribly restless and felt she wanted to get away from the Casa de Rocha. 'I – I won't stay for tea,' she said. 'I have a long drive back to the hotel, and later this evening I shall be leaving for London to rejoin my aunt—'

'Is that prospect so exciting that you cannot spare ten minutes for refreshment in my house?' Though that caustic little smile was at the edge of the Duque's boldly shaped lips, his eyes had narrowed so that the very dark lashes concealed their expression. He gestured with a lean, darkly tanned hand, indicating that Jaine be seated in one of the upright chairs. 'Come, all Brazilian drivers are swift, so you will not arrive too late to catch that all-important plane. Sit down, *senhorita*, and do try to relax . . . after your ordeal.'

Jaine gave him a rather uncertain look . . . it seemed not to show at all that he had just been told that his marriage was off. Was it pride that masked his feelings? Or had he

31

not cared deeply enough for Laraine to be really troubled that she had sent her poor plain cousin to tell him he was jilted?

It was a tricky situation, and though every fibre of Jaine's being was longing for escape from his presence she found herself obeying his order that she sit down. Even as she did so there was a discreet tap on the door, which then opened to admit the manservant with the tea tray. He brought it to the table beside Jaine's chair and then withdrew from the room, leaving her, presumably, to do the honours.

'I take coffee,' said the Duque, taking at the same time a nearby chair and stretching out those long booted legs.

'With cream, *senhor*?' She held the silver coffee-pot as she glanced at him, and felt a nerve flutter in her throat. It wasn't often that she was called upon to pour coffee for a man . . . least of all one who looked and behaved as masterfully as the Duque Pedro de Zanto.

'Coffee . . . black as my soul,' he said, quizzically, almost outrageously, so that Jaine quickly lowered her gaze and poured the dark, aromatic Brazilian coffee into one of the beautiful porcelain cups, set in a gold-fluted saucer with tiny bluebirds painted in flight on the translucent china.

After Jaine had handed the Duque his black, strong coffee, she poured a cup of tea for herself and added both cream and sugar.

'And you must eat one or more of the cakes,' he said. 'I am sure you are feeling hungry, for if my guess is a correct one you have been on edge all day about the message you were instructed to bring to me and you probably ate very little lunch. Am I right, *senhorita*?'

'I think that you know you're right, *senhor*.' Jaine sipped her tea, which was delicious, but even the drinking of tea could not dispel the strangeness of this interlude, nor could she quite suppress her feeling of apprehension. This man was of the ruling class, arrogant and self-assured, and full of pride. He wasn't going to let her get off so lightly for bringing unpleasant news to him. She felt sure that his lounging air was a pose and that something lay smouldering in his manner ... like a snake in the sun, getting ready to strike in its own good time.

'And how long, *senhorita*, have you been in Brazil?' he asked suavely.

'Only a few days. I came for the—' There she broke off and her eyes flicked his face, vivid as the edge of a dragonfly's wing. 'I am sorry the wedding is off, *senhor*. It will be a disappointment for your son.'

'And not for me?' He quirked one of those inordinately black brows and his facial expression was both mocking and interrogative. 'Think how attractive your cousin is – so blue-eyed, so warm-haired, so curvaceous and lively. Even as innocent as you are, you must have some conception of what it means for a man to have such a choice dish dashed from his lips?'

'But you said—' But once again the words died on her lips, for she was too untutored in the ways of men, and this particular man was more overwhelming in every way than those she had come into contact with as a secretary and niece to Madge Desmond. Madge's friends were worldly, but they were not primitive with it. They might be ruthlessly ambitious, but they were not really cruel ... as Jaine felt this Latin aristocrat could be.

'I know what I said, *senhorita*.' His well-marked lips curled around the words ... as a whip might curl around a female limb. 'I said to the devil with your cousin and I meant it. But,' he rose abruptly to his feet, towering above Jaine in the dark polished chair which had an inquisitorial hardness to it, 'you are quite right when you say that my son was looking forward to the novelty of an English girl at Goldenhawk, which is my true home some miles further along the coast. I proposed marriage to Laraine because she seemed the type with only the single qualification of being a decorative wife. I could not say to her "Come and live in my house and be a companion for my son", but I think I can say it to you, Miss Jaine Dare.'

His voice was too clear-cut, his words too explicit, and his English too cultured for Jaine to be mistaken in any way about what he had said to her.

And behind those explicit words lay an even deeper, sharp-cutting, very painful meaning. Laraine was so lovely that a man would have to marry her in order to escape scandal – and Jaine knew that in many ways these Latin people were rigidly circumspect – but it would not matter in the case of someone like Jaine. The Duque would not be expected to feel desire for a girl such as she, and so he could say to her:

'Come and live in my house . . . be my son's companion, for I shan't ever want you for my own.'

CHAPTER THREE

JAINE set aside her cup and saucer and rose to her feet. The Duque was so tall that she had to tilt her head in order to give him the full benefit of a look that scorned him and his suggestion. She might not seem much to him, but she had quite a bit of pride and this was in her eyes, her voice as she said to him, very clearly:

'The devil can take your proposition, *senhor*. I have a job already and I'm quite content with it, thank you.'

'Content,' he took her up, 'with being the poor relation in the household of a woman who lives mainly to please herself and to condone the flighty selfishness of a spoiled daughter? Ah yes, I know her to be spoiled and I was aware that she was marrying me to make a good match, but it was while in Portugal with my son we met her one day on the lawn of a friend's house, and she was so dazzling among that group of dark-haired Latin people that Tristao was enchanted by her and I thought – but that is water under the bridge!'

The Duque spread his hands in a very Latin gesture and shrugged the shoulders that were so wide and well-muscled under the fine white linen of his well-cut shirt.

'So, *senhorita*, you aren't pleased that I ask you to stay in my country and work for me? I had the impression that you were disenchanted with your role in the lives of your aunt and cousin – that of errand girl, tidying up in the wake of Laraine, and more or less threatened with dismissal if you did not come here today to do your cousin's dirty work – ah, you catch your breath and the green eyes grow wider if that is possible! I hit a nerve just then, *senhorita*.'

'Yes,' she admitted. 'I don't always like what I'm asked to do, but that doesn't mean that I'm going to leap at the bone you hold out to me.'

'Bone?' he quizzed. 'It seems to me to have a fair amount of meat on it, the chance I give you to live in one of the finest houses along this coast, as companion to a young boy who cannot run and play as actively as other children of his age. Don't you care for small boys, *senhorita*?'

She noticed how he phrased his questions, as if he felt it a waste of time for someone with her lack of looks to like big boys. She was very aware of seeming a mere stick of a woman to this very virile man.

'I'm not inhuman,' she said. 'I like children, but—'

'But you are too accustomed to paying duty on the charity received from your relations to obey an impulse involving a pair of strangers, and despite my engagement to your cousin I am a stranger to you, eh?' He gazed down at Jaine with that penetrating look of his, questing and dominating . . . and demanding.

'Very much a stranger, *senhor*, in a country strange to me.' She forced her gaze away from his and glanced at the panelled double doors that led to freedom from this house of surprises. 'I think I must be on my way, Your Excellency. As I have told you I have a plane to catch in just a few hours—'

'Don't catch it,' he said peremptorily. 'Start to live your own life, Jaine Dare – I dare you!'

Jaine stood frozen, fighting not to look at him. To see again that charisma that would be dangerous to an attractive woman, let alone one like herself, whose lonely heart had taught itself not to reach out for a dream because it could never take on the lovely warmth of reality. If she dared to go to Goldenhawk she would be cutting herself loose from the half-loaf for a wildly exotic fruit that might turn bitter to her taste. No! Her life with Madge could never break her heart . . . but from the first moment she had looked at the Duque Pedro she had known that he might break hers.

'I thought you might have courage,' there was an acid-sweet mockery to the smile he bent upon her, 'from the way you undertook to carry out an unpleasant duty for your cousin. But I see that your courage quails at the thought of freedom and sunlight and the beauty of the tropics. You disappoint me, Miss Dare!' He stepped aside from the doors and flung out a hand in a gesture of dismissal. 'Be off with you, go back to your life of being doormat to the Desmonds.'

Doormat! Jaine's temper flared and if she could have reached for that dark cruel face she would have slapped, clawed, caused him a little of the pain that other people had no conscience in causing her.

'I'd be no more than that in *your* household,' she flung at him.

'On the contrary – as companion to *my* son, Miss Dare, you would have the most responsible position of your life. Tristao is of the greatest importance to me, a child with a brave young heart in a body much hurt when he was only an infant. You would have to guard his person and his welfare and that would automatically place you in a position very much above that of a secretary-cum-maid to a popular actress of no great merit as a performer. Your salary would be an excellent one, you would have your own suite of rooms at Goldenhawk, and hours of work cognizant with the requirements of one small boy instead of a pair of female relatives with little regard for you, or anyone else. Well, do I make myself clear, *senhorita*?'

'Clear as plate glass, *senhor*.' Jaine, for her sins, had a sense of humour which had saved her time and time again from either a wickedly Irish-Huguenot display of temper, or a heart-racked bout of lonely weeping. 'But isn't this all rather sudden?' she asked. 'You know nothing of me apart from my relationship to Laraine. Setting aside the fact that I don't resemble her in the smallest degree, it could well be that I have an equally self-inclined nature. I might not be at all the proper person to have charge of your son and heir.'

'That is very true,' he agreed, and suddenly he stepped

towards her and before she could elude his touch or his intention he had taken the point of her chin into the hard grip of his fingers and was tilting her face to the light streaming in through the *sala*'s long windows. With unsparing eyes he examined every facet of her face, raking his gaze over her facial bones; her pale, clear, unpainted skin, the sensitive shape of her mouth, the fey and the obstinate in her features. Then abruptly, almost shockingly, his eyes were looking directly into hers . . . and it was as if that look was a touch that ran all down her spine and shot into her bones a series of sensations she had never felt or suffered in her life before.

'There is something of Ephyre about you . . . the constant nymph, forever evading a revelation of your true self in case you are betrayed. With the Desmonds you can give service without giving your heart . . . with a child it might be different, and you are very much afraid of love, are you not?'

'That – that is none of your business—' She tried to twist away from his scrutiny, but he held her relentlessly. 'It would be foolish for someone like me to be – romantically inclined.'

'And may I ask why?'

'You are looking right at me, *senhor*, so I imagine you see the reason for yourself.'

'You mean, of course, that you are no beauty?'

'I am what my cousin once called me – an ugly duckling.'

'And you were young, impressionable, and hurt by that?'

'I – I knew it to be the truth. In the house of an actress there are many mirrors, *senhor*.'

'*Diabo*,' the word whispered from his lips, 'but of course, and so you accept the mirror reflection of yourself and creep a little every day into the shell of the dutiful, uncomplaining, efficient spinster, secretary and niece. *Senhorinha*,

38

do you really suppose that the companion of a child has of necessity to be a picture of candy-box prettiness?'

'You did say that your son was dazzled by my cousin,' Jaine reminded him, and was amazed at her stoicism in the face of the blunt truth from his clear-cut lips. For a Latin he had a remarkable command of English words and he knew how to apply them to the fullest effect. He made her see with shocking clarity the person she was turning into . . . dull, dutiful, tucked into the background of other people's far more exciting lives. And it suited Madge to have her that way. Efficient, reliable, and drab, who despite her youth was in no way a source of competition when men came to the Westminster flat and drank cocktails.

'Are you afraid,' asked the Duque, 'that Tristao will not be so impressed by you?'

'I should think he'll be very disappointed if you land him with a plain companion when he expected a pretty mother.'

'Won't you put it to the test and see how he reacts?'

'I – I can hardly place my head on that sort of chopping-block, *senhor*. I have to work for my living and half a loaf is better than no bread at all.'

'Tell me,' his hard fingers slid away from her face and he straightened to his full height, 'do you have to return immediately to London?'

'My passage is booked on the midnight flight—'

'It can be cancelled,' he said decisively. 'A wire can be sent to your aunt to say that you are a trifle unwell and are advised to remain another week in Porto de Zanto. You have money?'

'Hardly – Madge paid up the bill until I leave tonight, and arranged the transfer of my flight ticket. As I live with my aunt I receive only a token wage.'

'*Diabo!*' he said again. 'Really monstrous and quite fool-hardy of you to accept such a situation. I thought Latin matriarchs could be hard enough on female relatives, but this actress is even beyond my experience!'

'Don't forget,' Jaine dared to say, 'that she almost became your mother-in-law.'

'And don't you forget,' he rejoined, 'that I am not a youthful English girl with an abundance of patience, charity, and self-denial. I warned Laraine that I would accept no interference from her mother ... *por deus*, that is all over with, and we talk, you and I, of this matter of arranging that you meet Tristao. Yes, I have decided! You will stay a week longer at Porto de Zanto and the matter of the hotel bills will be settled by me, and no argument, *senhorinha*. I have no patience with arguments that lead only to a conclusion already settled upon. If you see my son and if you find that you get along with him, will you agree to come to Goldenhawk?'

Even as Jaine would have argued with him, there shot right through her a dart of desire to accept his proposition. Even as the sensible side of her argued that the Duque was arrogant, and probably had a temper like a lash, she could not deny a stirring of excitement, the awakening of that wish (long thrust out of sight) to break free of Madge's domination.

Jaine glanced at the Duque and with her every instinct she knew that he would be more dominant, more hard to please, more subtle and extraordinary than anyone she had ever met.

'Why do you hesitate?' he asked. 'Don't you like the look of me?'

Nerves fluttered in her stomach when he said that ... it would be a passport to no-man's-land to like the look of Pedro de Zanto. 'I should like to meet your son, *senhor*, but I – I don't like the idea of accepting money from a stranger – to pay my hotel bill if I stay another week.'

'Independent as well, eh?' He pushed his hands into the pockets of his breeches and his regard became slightly indolent, as if the time to threaten and the time to persuade had passed for now. 'Well, be assured that I shan't pay your bill with my cheque and thereby make the tongues of Porto de Zanto wag. At the end of the week, when you will have met Tristao and made your decision, I shall give you the cash and you will call it a small salary in advance, or wages in lieu of notice. Does that set your mind at ease?'

Jaine flushed slightly, for in his eyes she could see those wicked glimmers of male amusement at the idea of people gossiping about him and herself. A man such as he would always have had the most attractive women at his beck and call ... she knew now that Laraine had run out on him because he was too blasé about women to place her upon the pedestal she craved for.

Jaine lowered her gaze and wondered in that moment who had been the mother of his son and why the Duque had not married her.

'Well, now you are not going to dash back to the hotel in order to catch your plane, I suggest, *senhorinha*, that you be seated again and finish your tea.'

'My driver is waiting,' she said uncertainly.

'Your driver is taking refreshment at this precise moment and is quite happy. Relax, Miss Dare. I am going to leave you for a while in order to write a letter – please to eat the cream cakes, for I don't imagine that you need to watch your figure in case it gets out of hand.'

With these words, and with a suave bow he withdrew from the *sala* and closed the carved doors behind him, leaving Jaine to stare at them, as if she still saw imposed upon the shining wood an image of that tall, dark, demanding figure.

She sat down in obedience to a sudden tremor in her legs. Was it really possible that in a single hour she had allowed her life to be turned topsy-turvy by a total stranger? Her throat felt dry and she poured herself some more tea and quickly drank it. The sun came through the windows and flickered on the surface of the silver pot and she stared at the flicker as if hypnotized. No! It would be madness to do as he asked ... as he ordered. What did she know about children? Her life had been taken up with the demands of an actress ... do this, do that, and don't argue, my girl, unless you want to find yourself out on your ear!

Almost unaware Jaine picked up a cake fork and took a mouthful of the delicious confectionery. She half-closed her eyes, rather like a thin young cat tasting cream, and she visualized Madge's face if and when her age-old threat was turned against her and it was her humble and despised niece who gave notice that she was quitting .. leaving the Westminster ménage to become an employee of the Duque Pedro.

Jaine's eyes were a brilliant green against the frightened and yet excited pallor of her face. Dare was her name and it would be very daring of her to break the bonds of habit and duty, so imposed upon her that even in this moment she felt their mark. Back in London she had hesitated to break free because all that had loomed had been the prospect of a routine office job and the dullness of a bedsitter in a London back street ... but now, out of the blue, out of the gold of a tropical afternoon, she had been offered a well-paid post in a ducal household, here in a land so strange and new and exotic.

In some surprise she found herself half-way through her second cake. She had been hungry! Hungry for so many things.

She was standing at the long windows, gazing out at the Brazilian palm trees, so aloof, fronded and savage, when she caught a sound that swung her to face the double doors, almost with bated breath. They were pushed open and there was the Duque again. This time he was clad in an impeccable dark-grey suit and in place of that almost untamed virility there was a look of total distinction; a dark nobility of feature and person.

'The sun is going down the sky,' he said, 'and I see that

you are now quite ready to leave. I shall, some time tomorrow, telephone you at the hotel and let you know when you can meet my son. This is agreed? You are content with the arrangement?'

'Content is not quite the word, *senhor*, but I am interested in the post that you offer me. It would make quite a change for me, if it turns out that I meet with your son's approval.'

'Will you arrange to send that wire to Mrs. Desmond, or shall I?' He seemed to regard her with abrupt sternness, accentuated by the immaculate, stone-coloured suit, beneath which was a pale-grey shirt with a fine silk stripe. His tie was such a dark purple it was almost black, and it was tied with only the perfection that a valet could achieve.

'I must send the wire myself,' said Jaine. 'I must have the nerve to do it.'

'I think you have nerve,' he said. 'More than you perhaps realize yourself. And now, *senhorinha*, I will see you to your car and say *adeus* for now.'

With an air of composure Jaine walked towards him, and each step seemed as if it drew her into his dark-lashed, tawny-irised eyes. She felt acutely the vitality and the command of the man, and she knew how hard it was for any woman to resist a man who made her feel to the marrow of her bones the fact that she was a woman. Oh lord, he had such a decisively chiselled, darkly foreign face, and his intent appraisal from the rather slanting eyes made her feel defenceless. There was challenge and danger in the man, and they seemed to reach out to her. There were raven glints in his hair, and she clung to her composure for all she was worth.

With casual, almost animal grace he stood aside for her to precede him into the corridor that had grown flame-shadowed as the sun began to decline. As he walked at her side to the staircase he seemed very tall and overpowering . . . and yet she felt that in some way he was intrigued by the riddle of her. She probably had a simplicity and a candour he found unusual . . . perhaps childlike.

It could well be that a young woman of twenty-two who had not yet been in love, or attracted love, was in some ways still an adolescent. Perhaps it was that in her which made him see her as the ideal companion for his young son?

He came with her right to the door of the car. '*Adeus, senhorinha.*' His deep voice seemed to go right through her. 'Send that wire and await my telephone call, and don't be persuaded by your over-active sense of duty that you owe any more of your youthful devotion to your aunt. I imagine she has been refunded well above the initial outlay on your keep and education. Be tranquil, Miss Dare. Try, at least.'

Jaine entered the car, the door was closed, and only a few seconds later that tall figure was left behind on the steps of the Casa de Rocha. Still feeling tremulous and a trifle dazed, Jaine sank back against the leather of her seat and as the car sped along beneath the deep shadow of the driveway trees she let her mind wander back and forth over the incidents of the afternoon.

Darkness lay over the interior of this coastal town, and the lights of the harbour were blazing into the water when Jaine arrived back at her hotel. She went to the desk and told the clerk that she would not be leaving that night and wished to retain her room for the remainder of the week. She asked that her flight to Rio be cancelled, and also her flight to England, and requested that a wire be sent to London. She didn't quite obey the Duque in the message she sent, for the dash of Irish in her veins made her rather superstitious. The message which went was short and to the point: 'Feel like a short holiday. All okay matter of Laraine.'

Well, that was that, and if Madge kicked up a fuss Jaine would not be there to endure one of those theatrical bouts of temper for which her aunt was famous.

44

Jaine proceeded to her hotel room, where she slung her handbag to the bed, kicked off her shoes and did a small dance of bravado on the fluffy carpet.

This was the first time she had really defied Madge, and as she drifted to her balcony to gaze down at the harbour lights, strung along the rigging of the sea-craft moored there, and making pools of shadowy gold along the sea-walls, she felt a sense of amazement that she of all people should allow a man to persuade her to be rebellious for the first time in her life.

And what a man! As she saw her own thin young face reflected in the glass of the balcony doors she caught her breath. She was so utterly a novice when it came to men, and the Duque was so worldly, wealthy, and vitally attractive. He knew exactly how to bend a woman to his will . . . how to captivate when he so wished, and how to let go with a shrug of his shoulders if the woman didn't quite measure up to his requirements.

Jaine felt quite certain that her wire would infuriate Laraine. Her cousin had probably had visions of the Duque running after her, and giving chase in that private plane Laraine had mentioned. Although Laraine had not taken to the stage like her mother, there was a dramatic streak in her, and Jaine knew that she would have revelled in being pursued by her Latin fiancé. She might have had that in mind all along; her flight might have been meant as a challenge to the Duque, to have him show that she meant far more to him than a mere mother for his son by another woman.

Well, Laraine, for once in her spoiled life, was in for a disappointment, and if it turned out that Jaine hit it off with Tristao, then the roof was going to blow off the flat at West-minster when her aunt and her cousin were informed that she was actually going to work for the man Laraine had chosen to play about with.

A smile quivered on Jaine's lips . . . had Laraine really thought that she could treat Pedro de Zanto as if he were the gangling and good-natured Billy Hopgood? When Laraine had run out on Billy he had probably been lachrymose, but the Duque had snapped his fingers and consigned her to the devil.

Jaine dragged her thoughts back to the present and glanced at her wristwatch. It was almost time for dinner, so she had better snap out of her day-dreaming and get ready for the evening meal, which in accordance with Brazilian protocol was always fairly late and served in the restaurant downstairs, where a small orchestra played and where couples danced. Jaine didn't feel particularly shy about sitting alone. She was accustomed to her own company, and on trips with Madge she was often left to eat alone while her aunt, in her role of the glamorous actress, dined with new or old acquaintances.

It rarely took Jaine very long to complete her toilette. After a shower and a quick change into one of her simple dresses, she had only to run a comb through her monk's cap of hair, skim a powder-puff over her nose, and descend to the dining-room, to take her corner table. She took up the menu, but it was some minutes before a waiter came to take her order. She didn't really mind that she seemed so unnoticeable, but she couldn't help but wonder what it would feel like to dine with someone like the Duque Pedro. She felt quite certain that he would be treated like royalty, and the girl with him like a princess. The waiters would bow all over him, the best wine would be produced, and every female eye in the room would be upon his face and his person.

Jaine nibbled a breadstick and her smile had a hint of the Mona Lisa about it ... though she would have been surprised if someone had intimated this.

So after all she was staying a while at Porto de Zanto; she would be able to explore and bathe in the sapphire sea ... and see what Destiny had in store for her with regard to the Duque and his son.

All the next day Jaine waited around the hotel for the Duque's telephone call, but he didn't ring her and she went to bed wondering if he had had second thoughts about arranging a meeting between her and the boy.

When she awoke the following morning, after a somewhat restless night, she had the feeling that she was going to be let down. People made promises on the spur of the moment, and then discarded them as casually as fluff from a sleeve, and after checking her money Jaine found that she had sufficient for one more day at the hotel; she didn't have to rely on the uncertain good grace of a man she didn't really know.

She took breakfast on her balcony, *croissants* spread with honey, and two cups of coffee, and she made pretend she was a well-off tourist who had no need to worry about earning her living. The sun felt beautifully warm and she decided to take a stroll round the Port of Zanto and later on to spend some time on the soft white sand of the beach. She was so accustomed to her negative role in life that she held out no real hope that the Duque would remember that for a brief hour he had met her and considered if she might be a suitable companion for his son.

Jaine gave a slight shrug and resolved not to waste another day at the hotel when she could see something of the harbour and the town, and maybe take a ride in one of the open carriages that plied their trade along the seafront.

She packed a swimsuit and a towel into a bag, and clad herself in cabin-boy pants in a cat-green colour (a rather daring buy which she had concealed from Madge) and topped them off with a white cuffed shirt. With her hair combed smooth, and her face as God had made it, she looked rather like a boy. A youth with delicate limbs and eyes both candid and uncertain of people. A grin came and went on her lips as she studied her reflection in the mirror of the wardrobe. She could have gone as a cabin-boy on one of the yachts in the harbour and there would have been no one

47

to really care what became of her.

Looking back down the years she could not remember a single sign of real affection from anyone. As a child she had cried alone when she felt miserable; there had been no warm kisses lavished on her childish hurts: no murmurs of comfort during her adolescent trials.

She stared into her emerald eyes in the mirror and thought how true it was that one's childhood shaped the adult that one became. It had been clever of Poe to pen the lines that sprang to her mind in that bedroom of a hotel on the Brazilian coast:

> 'From childhood's hour I have not been
> As others were – I have not seen
> As others saw – I could not bring
> My passions from a common spring.'

CHAPTER FOUR

JAINE escaped from her hotel bedroom into the sunshine, and for the next few hours she rambled about Porto de Zanto.

She was *sozinha* again, and enjoying it. She wandered along the Rua das Claras and admired the many strange and colourful things in the shop windows; she saw unusual gems and medals attached to fine silver and gold chains, and coveted a jewel-case carved from tortoiseshell into the shape of a shell and decorated by a single large topaz, winking as it caught the sunlight like a brilliant tawny eye. Jaine sighed, for she couldn't afford to buy the really pretty things of life, and had an inborn distaste for what was specious and cheap.

She strolled on, for it did no good to sigh for things she couldn't have, and she climbed the streets that were sloping and antiquely cobbled, leading into quaint squares in which stood fountains and palm trees, and where from the balconies of high-up windows bright plants spilled from terracotta pots.

Never had Jaine seen a place so warm-coloured, so filled with scent and sunlight and richly evocative shadow. No matter what political upheavals might be going on elsewhere in this Latin country, here at least there was a rich, languorous air of peace, as if the people of Porto de Zanto liked their way of life and were content that things should remain as they were.

Jaine sat on a sea-wall and ate big shrimps from a bag, just purchased from one of the fishermen wearing a black waistband in place of a belt, and looking not unlike a Moorish pirate. They had understood each other with signs. Jaine had pointed to the shrimps, and then to her lips, and produced her purse. A wide grin had split his mouth, revealing a set of gleaming white teeth, and because he had not looked her over from head to foot in the way of Latin men, she had assumed that he thought her a boy, and the thought amused her again as she sat enjoying her shrimps, and the little eddies of tangy breeze that blew up the slope of the beach.

Worn steps led down to the beach and later on, she promised herself, she would go for a swim in that blue water, changing into her swimsuit behind one of those fantastic rocks like altar pieces to the sea-gods.

The shrimps were delicious, and so much bigger and sweeter than those to be bought in England at a much higher price. Like a young cat on a sunlit wall Jaine enjoyed her shellfish and felt as if she had escaped off a leash for a short time. She watched lazily as the fishermen unloaded their painted boats, bringing off the colourful catches of red mullet, bonito, small rainbow fish, and the tentacled octopus, all of which would be used in the spicy dishes served in the attractively run-down harbour restaurants.

She was drowsing there when she noticed an old woman selling fruit from a basket and Jaine went over to her and selected a *fruta do conde* for her dessert; the tasty custard-apple which was like biting into a fruit made entirely of thick vanilla ice-cream.

Back home Jaine would have felt too inhibited to eat like this in the street, but here, as if like Dorothy she had followed a yellow brick road to enchantment, she bit into the fruit and was careless of being watched. Even unaware that as a youthful stranger with a very white skin she was observed and presented a picture of a slim, effeminate boy, with a shy-proud head capped by seal-smooth hair; with a straight young back and long legs.

She was seated thus, the sun and the sea merging to make a clear image of everything around her, when she saw a small child dart into the road that curved down from the residential part of the town. A scarlet ball ran across the road and was pursued by the small boy, while at the same time a

50

big car came smoothly downhill and gave every sign of turning the corner in time to hit the child.

Jaine tossed aside her partly eaten custard-apple and ran swiftly in the direction of the boy, her arms scooping him up in the very path of the car, the brakes of which were immediately applied so that the vehicle hissed to a halt only a small distance away from Jaine and her small, startled burden.

That clear sea-light etched the scene with startling clarity ... the slim figure in cabin-boy pants holding tightly a little figure with dark curly hair ... and the long grey car, its driving door flung wide to give exit to a tall, violently angry man.

'By the grace of Fate!' His voice struck at Jaine like a whiplash. 'What the devil are you doing?'

'I – I should think that was obvious,' she rejoined breathlessly. 'The kiddy was chasing his ball and he didn't see your car—' She turned around with her plump young burden, who was now struggling and bawling for his *avozinha*; the grandmother who came hurrying to join the crowd that was collecting in the centre of the road. Other cars were pulling to a halt and horns were adding their noise to the howls of the rescued child, who was torn between demands for his grandmother and his scarlet ball.

For Jaine the next few minutes were chaotic; the excitable Latin people milled about her, thumping her on the shoulders to congratulate her courage in saving the little one, while others, with a respect that was forthright rather than humble, spoke to the Duque and said they had seen it all. He had not been driving too swiftly, it was that the little one had been unheeding of everyone in his desire to secure the beloved ball which had got away from him. 'The *turisto*, the *menio*, had with courage saved the child from a possible bad injury!' Jaine's hand was grabbed and shaken so hard by one of the fishermen that she thought her fingers would be dislocated. *Menio* – boy! Good lord!

Her sudden feeling of weakness must have communicated itself to the Duque, for the next instant she was taken secure hold of, and a minute later she found herself in a veloured seat of the grey car – with an imposing crest on the door – and the engine was being started up beneath the touch of the lean, dark, well-shaped hands.

Jaine sat very still as the immaculate, purring, well-sprung Bentley sped along the harbour road, leaving behind the cluster of fisherfolk who had quite simply taken her for a boy – not only from the way she was dressed, but by reason of her agility in quickly dashing to the rescue.

'Well,' said the Duque, 'I never thought that our second meeting could be even more dramatic than our first. How did you like being called a brave boy?'

Now that the clamour of her pulses had subsided some-what, and those shock-waves of surprise had settled down, Jaine could glance at the assertive profile with at least a look of coolness. 'I don't quite know what I feel,' she said. 'I'm only glad that I was on hand to stop the little boy from being hurt. You saw me, but on that curve you might not have noticed the child.'

'And do you still maintain, Miss Dare, that you lack cour-age?'

'One doesn't think about courage or cowardice on the spur of the moment. One obeys impulse or instinct.'

'Your instinctive liking for small things, eh?' There was a slightly indulgent note in the deep voice this time, and as he spoke he drove the car into the forecourt of one of those restaurants Jaine had noticed but had passed by on account of the lack of funds in her purse. She could have gone back to the hotel for lunch, but that would have added to her bill, and up until this moment she had not though to see any more of Pedro de Zanto.

'Have you eaten?' he inquired, turning to confront her, a grey-clad elbow on the leather wheel, and so overpoweringly close to her that she had either to endure the closeness, or shrink in her seat like a silly prude. Her nostrils tensed to a tangy fragrance emitted by his close-shaven skin, and to the aroma of fine cigar leaf. The man, like his car, was streamlined and aristocratic, with a faultless control that yet did not hide the ability to be lethal in dealing with a mere girl. His was an effortless and an ineffable charm, with a strong undercurrent of danger.

'I – I've had some shrimps and a custard-apple,' she said. 'They were most enjoyable, eaten there in the sunshine.'

'I'm sure they were.' His mouth arched at the corner, almost in a smile. 'But hardly filling for a girl not yet fully grown—'

'I'm twenty-two, *senhor*,' she broke in, half shocked to be taken first for a boy and now for an adolescent.

He stared at her, with a sardonic elevation of his black eyebrows. His eyes, that were translucent as fine sherry, flicked her hair, and then the slim pallor of her neck in the opening of her pale, flimsy shirt. 'You are still young for your years, to look at, anyway. *Senhorinha*, will you take lunch with me?'

'What, dressed like this?' She glanced down at herself. 'I'm wearing pants and hardly look the correct sort of companion—'

'And now that you mention that word – and please to look at me! – why are you wandering about when I asked you to await my telephone call at your hotel? I phoned at nine-thirty this morning and was informed that you had gone out, presumably to swim.'

'I waited all day yesterday for your call – and I was about to go swimming when I dived after that child instead.'

'I could not phone you yesterday as a business matter of some urgency cropped up – the best time to bathe, you know, is when the moon is high. There is nothing to outshine moon-track swimming. Have you never tried it?'

'Why, no, *senhor*.' She looked at him wide-eyed; so he had meant to phone her as promised, and there still seemed a chance that she wouldn't have to leave his country just yet.

'I think,' he said, with a deliberate look, 'that there are a number of things you have not yet tried. It is this lack of world experience which gives you such a youthful, unguarded look. The women who have given all have no need to guard anything. Come, as you are with me it is no matter to anyone that you are dressed so casually – so almost like a boy. I wonder – do you have a wish that you had been born a boy?'

'Perhaps.' She shrugged, and knew already that she was guarding her emotions against this man. 'If one has to be an orphan it is sometimes better to be a masculine one.'

'You think men have a hardier nature and are less likely to be hurt by life?' His eyes became quizzical as he regarded her, a ray of sunlight knifing through the car window to display the vulnerability of her face to him. 'Yes, you have much to learn, *menina*, and your first lesson is that you must never regret your feminine sex. Some day you will be shown by a man that he is very glad indeed that you are a woman.'

'Really?' She gave a crooked little grin. 'I was once informed by Madge that a friend of hers thought me as sexless as a brownie, which in my country is a kind of mythical elf that is seen but never heard; a performer of unpleasant tasks, who never asks of life more than a pin to see the peepshow.'

'So you are a myth and not real, eh?' And before Jaine could draw back from him and not have to endure the exquisite torture of his touch, the Duque curved a lean hand over her left shoulder and pressed his fingers into her bones, there under the thin material of her shirt. 'You feel as if you might be real ... ah, you flinch. Don't you like a man to touch you? Is the sensation a strange one?'

'Of course,' she said, trying to speak lightly, so that he wouldn't guess how acutely sensitive she was to his touch.

'As far as men are concerned I'm usually unnoticeable.'

'And at the age of twenty-two you have never been kissed?'

'No!' The word wasn't so much a prudish negation of the very idea of being kissed, as a gasp of shock that he should speak of such things. The unexpected question made her look at his lips, but nothing within her experience could give the faintest notion of what it would feel like to have that bold, sculptured mouth in possession of her untried lips.

'You know,' he said lazily, and then outrageously, 'you cannot catch a baby from being kissed.'

'I think,' she said shakily, 'that a look from you, *senhor*, might do the trick.'

'*Diabo*, the girl has a sense of humour which has not yet received the *coup de grâce* from the arrogant aunt! Come, we will go and eat, and then you will see Tristao.'

'Today?' Jaine gave him a surprised look.

'This very day, *Senhorina*. He is at the *quinta* of a friend of mine and our visit will be quite casual, with no indication as yet that you might become his companion. We don't want to disappoint him a second time, eh?'

'Indeed not,' said Jaine, but as she slipped from the car and stood in the sunlight of the forecourt of the Black Rose, as the restaurant was called, she could feel how much she wanted the job, and she could also feel against her shoulder bones the branding of his personality which the Duque had left there. She cast a swift glance at him as he stood supple in the sun, indolent, and yet with something almost like a shadow in his eyes. There, and then gone as he looked at her.

'It is good that I know, Miss Dare, that you would risk your life for a child, a small stranger to you. You are no doubt aware that the political situation in certain parts of Brazil is not all it should be, and I – well, it suffices to say that I don't always agree with certain policies in force at the present time. If you come to work for me—'

'I understand, *senhor*,' she said quietly. 'I promise to take great care of your son, if it should come about that he takes to me. I wonder if he will?'

'I wonder also, *menina*, but I will say again to you that you must drop this habit of thinking so little of yourself. No doubt you grew up wishing you looked like your cousin so life would be more indulgent towards you, but it is a fact that if you looked like her at this precise moment then you would not be entering a restaurant to eat with me.'

'You hate her that much?' Jaine glanced at his face as they entered the restaurant, where fans were turning in the whitewashed ceiling and where white-coated waiters were hurrying about with laden trays. There was a delicious aroma of spicy Latin food, and on a big side table a mound of tropical fruits.

'You cannot hate what you have never loved,' the Duque rejoined, and as he ended his clipped words the *patrão* of the Black Rose descended upon him, warm delight was voiced that he had chosen to lunch there, and without further ado they were escorted to a secluded table near a window, and with a snap of his fingers the *patrão* had summoned a waiter to take their lunch order and another to take their wine order.

'It is an honour, Excellency.' The *patrão* bowed again, and barely kept his alert dark eyes from sweeping over the slight, pants-clad figure of the Duque's companion. Jaine checked a grin. She must look odd beside the distinguished figure of Pedro de Zanto, and some of the other diners were looking at them with unconcealed curiosity. The Duque, however, seemed entirely unconcerned and was studying the wine list with the absorption of the connoisseur, having already ordered for both of them hot and cold *hors d'œuvres*, to be followed by the finest *filets* of steak with sliced onions, potatoes and peas.

'Do you like port?' he asked her abruptly. 'But perhaps you aren't acquainted with the sort I mean and have tasted

56

only that sickly red stuff served at English tables at the time of the Christmas festivities. Would you like to try a glass of real port?'

She nodded, and was very aware of being for the first time in her life a mild source of interest to a man who was possessed of a rare sort of magnetism. A man somewhat cynical, a whole lot ruthless, and filled to the brim with a vibrant masculinity. She felt that his courtliness had a slightly mocking edge to it, but somehow she didn't mind. It was a heady experience to see envy *of her* in the eyes of other women, even if that envy was mixed with amazement.

With a flourish the *hors d'œuvres* cart was wheeled to the side of the table and Jaine enjoyed the novelty of selecting whatever she fancied. Their port wine was uncorked, tasted and approved by the Duque, and then poured delicately pale gold into the deep bowls of the wine glasses, to shimmer there like melted amber.

'Lift your glass,' the Duque instructed her, 'and savour the wine's bouquet. The best of port is like the finest brandy, it must be warmed in the hand and its aroma must be savoured, so that one by one all the senses come into contact with it.' Then as he looked across at Jaine a brief smile showed the white gleaming edge of his teeth. 'Do I sound as if I am taking in hand your tuition as a woman of the world?'

'A little,' she said, 'but I don't mind. I am grateful that you should bother with me, and still rather amazed that you didn't have me thrown out of your house the other day. When I look back—'

'Never look back,' he chided her, his wine glass near his lips as he allowed the aroma of the port to steal to his nostrils. 'All the yesterdays are gone as if snuffed out like so many candles; a little of their smoke might linger to fog the mind and cloud the heart, but it is always better to look forward. Drink your wine, *senhorinha*, and eat your food.'

She obeyed him, and thought over his remark about the smoke of a snuffed-out yesterday clouding the heart. Did he care so much for his son because he had deeply loved the mother? Why, then, had he not made her his wife? What could have happened that had caused Tristao to be born out of wedlock?

Jaine was deeply intrigued, and somehow it was no longer possible for her to think of Pedro de Zanto as a wealthy rakehell who had played around with a woman, and then made tardy recompense by adopting the boy he had caused to be born. No, there was a lot more to the story than that . . . and a whole lot more to the Duque. Jaine, so sheltered in her personal life, so curiously untouched by the intrigues of Madge Desmond, was not so innocent that she didn't know – there in the Black Rose, as the golden port ran warm through her veins – that she was dangerously close to falling headlong in love for the first time in her life. The only way to escape such a fall would be to leave Porto de Zanto today; meet Pedro's son because she had promised, and then say afterwards that she didn't feel right about leaving Madge in the lurch. Yes, it might be wiser to grasp at that straw in the event that Tristao liked the idea of having an English *confianca*.

'So this morning you have seen something of the town?'

Jaine gave a start as the words cut into her thoughts . . . as that deep voice, resonant, cultured, mercilessly attractive, cut down like cornstalks the resolves she had been sowing. As she looked at him her head swam with the strong wine, and she felt acutely at the mercy of the tawny eyes deep in dark lashes. Her heart shook in case he realized what was happening to her . . . nothing, past or since, would be more mortifying than to have him guess that already she was more than half in love with him . . . *she*, unfledged, undesired, unadorned!

'What is it?' His voice dropped into a deeper note. 'You

look afraid.'

'I – it's the wine,' she said quietly. 'I'm not accustomed to it and it's making my head float.'

'I see.' A smile flickered across his lips. 'I am leading you a little too quickly into the baptismal fires of life and you are afraid that I shall take advantage of your ineffable innocence. Take heart, here comes our steak, and that will soon offset the effects of the port.'

Jaine smiled slightly, for she welcomed his mockery, his little digs at her youthful inadequacy as a woman. She could defend herself against his mockery, but not against the pity he might feel for a plain little fool in love with him.

The steak was delicious, the onions cooked to a golden brown, and never before had Jaine tasted baked sweet potatoes in pepper gravy with tiny sweet peas.

This was indeed her baptismal . . . a plunging head first into contact with a magnetic man, deep as the sea, and yet frankly fond of the good things of life. While they ate their meal, and then drank dark Brazilian coffee, he talked about the Port of Zanto, and admitted that he was a direct descendant of the Duque Pedro who had loved one of the Wailing Doves who had been carried off by pirates and ransomed with gems.

'The story intrigues you as a romantic one, eh?' The Duque leaned back in his seat and studied Jaine. 'It is strange, but there is generally a touch of savagery in anything truly romantic, as if it has to be tested by steel or fire. Are you wondering, *menina*, at the irony of a rather cruel *duque* feeling a love beyond rubies for a gentle nun? The story might be too unreal for believing if it were not for the fact that it is a true one. My ancestor ransomed his true love, but even so she would not renounce her vows, and so he married someone else for the sake of the heritage, a vast one in those far-off days, stretching to the shores of the Amazon and beyond them. A *duque* in those days had the powers of his absent Portuguese king, for whom he had sailed and

plundered the new world for the old, gold one. Today—'
Pedro de Zanto made an explicit gesture with his hand; the
right hand on which gleamed a gold ring crested by a golden
hawk. Jaine had noticed the hawk while the lean hand had
toyed with a wine glass during the course of lunch. So detailed, so perfectly incised in the gold that it must have been
worked by a master craftsman many years ago, perhaps for
the man who had loved a nun.

'Today,' he repeated, with a deceptive softness of steel
cutting its way through silk, 'there are factors at work more
cruel because men pretend to be more civilized. Ah well,
such things are not for the ears of a young girl, and now we
have lunched we must be on our way to my friend, the Senhora Felicia de Evangel, who was nurse to my sister before
her marriage to Castro de Evangel, the well-known poet.
She and Castro are without children of their own and Felicia
enjoys the company of Tristao. For some reason he does not
like the Casa de Rocha, and so when I come to the coast on
business I let him stay with Felicia. Tell me, did my *casa*
strike you as a rather forbidding place, *senhorinha*?'

'Well – yes,' Jaine admitted, intrigued by all that he had
told her about the woman they would soon be on their way to
see. 'It is a house that suits its name. Madge called it a
fortaleza.'

'Ah, did she?' His eyes glittered. 'No doubt she thought
that I was going to keep shut up there her charming daughter, my prisoner of passion, never to be allowed out to dazzle
the eyes of other men. It will be amusing, no, if you come to
work for me?'

'It will probably make my aunt so mad that she'll want
nothing more to do with me,' said Jaine ruefully. 'I don't
know that I'm being very wise—'

'Where is the wisdom in being the scapegoat of a female
tyrant?' he asked, and into his eyes came a look of sardonic
inquiry. 'Do you suspect that I shall be even more of a
tyrant?'

Jaine gazed at him with candid eyes and saw again all that fascinated her about his face ... and all that terrified her. 'I'd be a fool if I took you for an easy-tempered man, *senhor*. Somehow I don't think that you endure fools too easily.'

'I don't,' he agreed, 'but let me make clear to you, Miss Dare, that though I consider you somewhat foolish to place any faith at all in the affections of your aunt and cousin, I do not regard you as an empty-headed female without the basic good sense to adapt yourself not only to the ways of my country but to the rules of my household. Goldenhawk is a country house, and the amusements of a town are some miles distant, and if I thought you were, in the old-fashioned term, a flapper, then I should be less than wise to invite you there.'

'Yet,' Jaine knew what she was going to say and was daring the devil by saying it, 'you must have known that my cousin – that Laraine was used to the high life.'

'I invited Laraine to be my wife, and as such she would have had to subdue her inclination to be the belle of the beach and the ballroom.' As he spoke, as he studied Jaine, his tawny eyes became almost cruel with mocking lights. 'You must be thankful that I shall have less jurisdiction over you – as a *confianca* – than I should have had over my bride.'

'If I come to work for you,' said Jaine, too accustomed to Madge's frankness to flinch from the Duque's, 'I have yet to pass muster with your son, and if I thought that he couldn't like me, then I wouldn't take the chance on working so far from England. It would be a fool's game.'

'I imagine it would.' He snapped his fingers for the waiter, and as he paid the bill, Jaine couldn't help but reflect that even if Tristao liked her, she would still be playing a foolish game in placing herself in the household of Pedro de Zanto, where she would see him every day, and fall ever deeper under his strange and mocking spell.

They left the restaurant followed by the curious glances of those who recognized the Duque but not his companion. Jaine knew there had been contempt in the women's eyes, for the way she was dressed, and for the boyish slimness of her figure. Also they would be wondering what had become of the Duque's glamorous girl-friend of the past few weeks, but none of them had dared to speak to him as he passed by their tables, his black head held high and his manner unapproachable.

Outside the day had grown even warmer, but the interior air-cooling system of the car had been switched on while they lunched and the veloured seat was not unbearably warm as Jaine slid into it. The door closed beside the Duque, and Jaine could feel the nervous beating of her heart as he swung the car out of the forecourt of the Black Rose and headed it along the sea road.

They had gone a couple of miles when the Duque abruptly broke the silence between them. 'Are you feeling nervous?' he asked.

'A little,' she admitted.

'It isn't so bad to meet a child, is it?' There was a note of irony in his voice. 'I imagine Laraine told you that I have never been married, and that Tristao was born out of wedlock? As you are obviously a young woman of idealistic notions this might worry you—'

'If you mean, *senhor*, would I hold it against a child that his father had an affair, then I can assure you that I wouldn't! My concern is that he'll think me a let-down after Laraine. She is so very pretty, and I have no illusions about my own looks. As Tristao is your son, *senhor*, he will have inherited quite a few of your likes and dislikes.'

'He is most certainly a boy of Zanto blood,' the Duque drawled, 'but have I given the impression that I dislike you?'

'As someone who may enter your employ I don't expect you to have any personal feeling for me. It's enough that you think me efficient, trustworthy, and not too much the coward.'

'You could never be called a glutton for admiration, could you?' His tone of voice was illimitably mocking, with also a tinge of curiosity to it. 'You know, *senhorinha*, it might intrigue a man of affairs to suddenly find himself with a girl who has never indulged in one. There is something curiously enticing about *"A garden enclosed . . . a spring shut up, a fountain sealed."* Are you acquainted with the Song of Solomon?'

'I – I may have read it at some time or other.' Jaine was confused by him as never before, and was inclined to ask herself if there was a chance that her innocence – it could only be called that – was likely to bring out the wolf in the Duque Pedro Almanzor de Ros Zanto.

'Why, just look!' she exclaimed. 'Isn't that rather enchanting?'

He glanced at the hillside chapel to which she was pointing, built high on a ledge of rock, washed in white, with its belfry enclosed in a narrow, open tower. Seated there, so utterly remote and peaceful, it was a perfect thing, to be imprinted on the mind and remembered.

'The Chapel of the Wailing Doves,' murmured the Duque. 'The old building was razed by fire a long time ago, but that one was built in its place and it does have a mystic air. And, of course, it keeps alive the old legend I was telling you about.'

'The bells must sound lovely when they chime for Angelus.'

'Indeed they do,' he said, rather dryly. 'Are you fascinated by the bells and beads, the prayers and chastity of the enclosed life? If so, then you will sympathize with my sister who entered a convent in Portugal several years ago. She was my only sister, and she chose the life after her *namorado* was killed while in Peru. He was an archaeologist, and he and his group had uncovered an ancient Inca burial

63

chamber, the roof of which collapsed before he could make his escape. It was said that the temple burial chamber was under the protection of the old gods, who took their revenge when Mateus and his team invaded the holy place. You might be intrigued that the pagan and the pure play such a part in the lives of my family.'

As the Duque spoke he swung the Bentley between the tall gate-posts of a private dwelling-place, which Jaine guessed to be the *quinta* of his friend the Senhora Felicia de Evangel. The gardens appeared, formal and carefully adorned by clipped hedges of bauhinia, with marble statuary and seats white in the sun against the velvety green of the lawns, and the gold and scarlet of the flower beds.

The car drew to a halt below curving steps that led to the house of dark-rose stone, with tall windows rising to the eaves that had an oriental tilt to them. The doorway was a fine baroque one, and at either side of the *quinta* there were charming staircases leading to a gallery encased in beautiful wrought iron.

The place had such an air of tranquillity and charm that it seemed to Jaine they could have been in the heart of Portugal itself. As she sat there, absorbed in admiring the house, the door beside her suddenly opened and a hand reached in to draw her from the car. As she felt that brown hand close on her own, as she was pulled forth into a shaft of sunlight, it was as if she were a new being, with a whole new set of sensations to feel and explore.

'Here we are, *senhorinha*.' His tawny eyes looked into hers, and his lip arched in that half-smile. 'I can feel you trembling a little. I can't recall that you trembled like this when you first confronted me.'

'That was different,' she said. 'I didn't enter your house hoping to win your approval. That would have been like trying to turn stones into strawberries – in the circumstances.'

'Quite,' he agreed, with a sardonic inflection, and a pain-

64

ful tightening of his lean fingers about hers. 'You expected a man's anger, which can be easier to face than a child's mercurial fancy. However, the moment has come to face it, and this time there may well be strawberries for tea!'

CHAPTER FIVE

THE large hall of the *quinta* was filled with an inviting coolness, where a number of flowers of different varieties were arranged in vases on attractive pedestals. At the centre of the hall was a staircase lined with *azulejos*, the smooth, indigo tiles from Portugal, on which were painted landscapes and figures. The furnishings had a dark gracefulness which Jaine noticed as a discreetly uniformed maid led herself and the Duque the length of the hall to a baroque archway leading out to a patio liberally hung with flowering creepers, with a fountain of *azulejos* playing in the sunlight.

Jaine caught her breath at the spicy mingling of scents in the enclosed garden, where she recognized a moonflower tree, the white and perfumed trumpets so waxen and still in the warm air. Bee-eaters and butterflies were on the wing among the trees, beneath which were graceful benches of white iron, wrought into the rococo patterns that were so striking in a Latin patio.

As the Duque's footfalls rang on the tiles, a woman arose from one of the benches and approached him with outstretched hands. Jaine saw at once that she was a woman of considerable attraction, with blue-black hair drawn back from a classic brow into a glossy chignon. Her skin was a a smooth, creamy olive against her dark hair, and she had fine Latin eyes that were smiling with that hint of mystery as she approached the tall figure of Pedro de Zanto.

Jaine was learning that the Latin races smile in a mysterious way, but rarely laugh aloud.

'*Meu caro*, what a delight to see you so soon again!'

The outstretched hands were taken into the Duque's, and each one was lightly saluted by his smiling lips. 'It is good to see you, *minha cara*. As always you are looking the ultimate pleasure to the eyes, and nowhere in Brazil is there a more delightful garden than yours. It is like a magical visit to Portugal itself.'

'You are gracious to say so, Pedro.' The Senhora de Evangel smiled up at him, her face like a Latin flower preening in the warmth of his smile. 'Castro is still away in that boat of his and so I have been doubly glad of the company of Tristao.'

Even as Jaine listened to this exchange, spoken in the perfect if slightly accented English used so frequently by educated Latins, she was aware of the boy seated like a gnome on one of the low and rambling walls about the patio. He stared straight at her without a hint of a smile in his eyes, which were like tilted flecks of gold in his puckish young face. Stretched beside him on the wall was a white cat, collared in blue with a bell attached, an indication that the animal was a bird-catcher, but all the same a beautiful creature whose purr could be heard as the boy caressed the sleek furry body.

Jaine and the child stared at each other, and her heart sank in case he should be hostile.

'Miss Dare!'

Jaine gave a start as the Duque addressed her, and as she swung her glance to him, her eyes were sheerest emerald in her slightly tortured face. The safe course, the wise decision, was no longer possible. She wanted to be with the Duque, and with his son. She wanted something intensely for the first time in her life, and it was rather terrible that her whole life seemed held in the small grubby hand of a boy stroking a white cat.

'Felicia,' he said suavely, as if he hadn't noticed that look on Jaine's face, 'this is the young woman about whom I telephoned you. She has a wish to work in Brazil, and we came by our meeting through the Dear Juan message which she brought me from her cousin. She is called Jaine.'

'I am pleased to know you, Miss Dare.' Felícia de Evangel looked directly at Jaine for the first time, and though her lips were curved into a smile, there was an intense look to her eyes as they searched, as Jaine knew, for some resemblance to Laraine, whom she would have seen or heard described as a dazzling Titian beauty. 'What has made you decide that you would like to work in Brazil, *senhorita*? As summer approaches the heat can be overpowering, and you are not the usual young Amazon that we see on our beaches, all nicely pork-red and peeling in the amazingly ugly bikini.'

Jaine hadn't dared to think what her reaction to Felicia de Evengel would be, for she looked too much the haughty Latin beauty to have a sense of humour. Her remark took Jaine by surprise, and then she just had to give way to her amusement at the picture of sunburnt, meaty young women on the tropical white beaches, all stretched out like so many sacrificial offerings in a couple of bits of muslin. Such a spectacle would strike Latin people as unpleasant, for they seemed to have an innate sense of dignity and an almost Renaissance love of beauty. Jaine recalled, at the same time, Laraine's preference for wearing one-piece bathing suits of form-fitting white sharkskin, stunning on her perfect figure.

No wonder ... her breath caught on her shy, slightly husky laugh. 'I am pleased to meet you, *senhora*,' she said to Felicia. 'You have the prettiest house I have ever seen in my life.'

'*Muito obrigado.*' The fine dark eyes grew warmer as they studied Jaine. 'It is not an historic house, for it was built only a decade ago, but it is rather nice and Portuguese in every detail. I am from Portugal, though my husband is Brazilian born like Pedro – like His Excellency.'

Felicia de Evangel glanced at the Duque as she said this, as if a trifle uncertain of how he regarded the cousin of his ex-fiancée. But he was standing there with his gaze upon his son and seemed not to have caught the note of inquiry in her voice. 'Come, Tristao, and meet a new friend. A young lady from England who may come to stay at Goldenhawk—'

'Why, are you going to marry her, Papa?' The clear young voice floated across the patio, above the sound of the fountain and the birds. For Jaine it was a devastating remark, one that rooted her to the spot, and yet made her want to run quickly away before she had to meet the Duque's eyes ever again.

'I thought,' the Duque said casually, 'that you would prefer to have the *senhorinha* for your very own English friend. Your *confianca* with whom you could explore the forest and take pony rides on the beach, and who would tell you all about her own country and accustom you to Anglo-Saxon ways before you grow up and go to school there – to my old school, *caro*.'

'Where you played Rugby, Papa?' The almost golden eyes looked gravely at the Duque, and Jaine felt certain that a tremor of pain ran through the tall, strong frame of the man who had seemed in such iron control of his emotions.

'Where, *caro*, you will be a far better scholar than I. I was a wild one and I had no English young lady to intrigue my mind with tales from books, as you will have. Come, my son, meet Miss Dare. Shake hands with her.'

The fountain water played in the short silence, and a brilliant blue bird darted with a slightly mocking whistle across the paved enclosure. Then, as the boy slid off the wall and came limping across the patio in obedience to his father, Jaine pulled herself together and formed her lips into a smile.

'How do you do, Miss Dare.' Tristao held out a hand to her, and raised to her a fawnish young face in which those gravely golden eyes were so oddly disturbing. She thought swiftly that he didn't really resemble the Duque, whose features were more striking than sensitive, and she decided at once that Tristao took after his mother.

'I'm glad to know you, Tristao, and I do hope we can be friends.' Jaine shook hands with him, and then felt a little stab of despair as the boy drew his hand away and didn't return her smile. He merely stared at her, and Jaine felt certain that he was comparing her to the image of her cousin on the velvety green lawn of a Portuguese house, probably clad in one of those deceptively simple flowered-chiffon dresses, bright hair catching the sunlight and looking not unlike a red-gold halo above the charming face.

Life for a child was made up of images, and it would seem unjust to Tristao that his father deprived him of Laraine's golden image and replaced it with one of a thin creature with sealskin hair and the green eyes of a cat.

Jaine, whose sense of humour had saved her soul on more than one occasion, broke into the wry smile that had something of the urchin in it, and something of the orphan.

'I see you're fond of cats,' she said. 'I like them, too, for dogs always seem big enough to bite off my head.'

'Papa has a wolfhound at Goldenhawk, so you would not care for him. He is almost as tall as Papa when he stretches up, and also there are pumas in the forest and sometimes they come to the very steps of the veranda.'

Well, thought Jaine, as much as she would have liked the job at Goldenhawk she wasn't going to beg for it. 'It must be interesting to live close to a wild forest,' she said, 'but I daresay a tame English girl like me would be better in her own country. I'd probably be petrified if I saw a puma.'

'They are just like big cats, really.' Tristao gazed intently into Jaine's eyes. 'I have never before seen a person with green eyes. Such eyes are usually seen only in cats—'

'Tristao,' the name came warningly from the lips of the Duque, 'you are forgetful of your good manners.'

'But they are so green, Papa.' A smile curled the boyish lips. 'I bet Miss Dare would purr if she was stroked.'

The remark was childish and Jaine was amused by it, but directly she saw the tightening of the Duque's face she said

70

quickly: 'You're quite right, Tristao. Would you like to try me?' She held out her slim arm to the boy. 'Stroke me and see.'

'You will do no such thing,' the Duque intervened. He glanced at Jaine and there seemed to be a strange glimmer of anger in his eyes. 'You must not encourage him to be disrespectful, Miss Dare. He must not imagine that a companion is an object of amusement; a kind of toy for him to disparage, or treat with the same inquisitiveness he would show his train set.'

'On the other hand, *senhor*,' she said, with a quiet firmness, 'I don't want Tristao to imagine that I'm an inhuman stick who has forgotten what it's like to be a child. Children are inquisitive, not only about their toys, but about the adults they come into contact with. I can't promise to be a Victorian prude of a companion for him, if that is what you require me to be. I can only be myself.'

The Duque frowned as he listened to her, his black brows joined in a decisive line above the bridge of his dominant nose. Tea things chimed on a tray as it was carried into the patio by a maid, and it was Felicia de Evangel who smoothed the troubled waters.

'Come, everyone! Tea is ready, and there are cream puffs and strawberry jam tarts.'

Strawberries! Jaine smiled tentatively at the Duque, and then saw the stern features relax. 'It would seem, Miss Dare, that you are far from being the placid young woman I should, perhaps, employ in the capacity of companion.'

'It is your prerogative, *senhor*.' She looked him in the eyes, chin uplifted, braving the decision that sent her far away from him, or kept her within his disturbing orbit. Being near to him would be even more tortuous than being miles away, for she knew that all he saw when he looked at her was a thin young person with eyes too big for her face and opinions which life with Madge and Laraine had not entirely quenched. They had not quite smothered

71

her spirit; that fey and rebellious spirit of her French-Irish inheritance.

'Yes, my prerogative,' he agreed suavely. 'And what do you say, Felicia? Does this green-eyed girl seem the stuff of which *confiancas* are made?'

'Pedro,' there was amazement as well as a hint of provocation in the look which Felicia gave him, 'it is unlike you to be unsure of a person's character. Miss Dare seems to me very young, but she also has a look of intelligence and imagination. I think those are qualities more important in a companion than—' The Senhora broke off, gave her charming smile, and commenced to pour out the tea. With a smile and without words she had conveyed the thought in her mind, that Jaine Dare was not pretty but was intelligent enough to give of her best to the right employer.

Yes, thought Jaine, with a touch of cynicism. It was the story of her life that she must accept with grace the crust of bread while the lovely Laraines and the gracious Felicias had the whole loaf to play with. A wry little smile quirked on her lips as Tristao sidled up to her and said in a stage whisper: 'Can you truly purr, *senhorinha?*'

As it happened, and it had something to do with the natural husky way which Jaine had of speaking, she could reproduce a sound in her throat which was amazingly purr-like. As she and Tristao paused near the fountain, where the tea-table was set, she bent her head to his and made that sound in her throat. At once he gave a laugh and his hand clenched around hers. 'And can you change yourself into one?' he queried, sotto voce.

'No, *amigo,* but I sometimes think it would be an advantage,' she said dryly.

The boy's eyes dwelt on her face, then suddenly he shot a look at his father, who was standing indolent in the sun, an eyebrow arched as he regarded Jaine with his son.

'I think, Papa, that I should like the *senhorinha* to come home with us,' Tristao announced.

'Oh, and why this sudden change of heart?' The Duque looked at the boy intently. 'A while ago you were telling Miss Dare that she would not be welcome at Golden-hawk.'

'Well – she is not so bad after all,' and then, as if inspired, and with a quick look that went all over Jaine, 'She has not been very well fed, I think, and could do with a home.'

'In which case we had better take her with us.' The Duque spoke dryly as his tawny eyes dwelt on Jaine, who was torn between consternation at Tristao's remark, and a stormy relief that the matter was settled and by the boy himself. Tristao wanted her, and the Duque had said all along that he would leave it to his son to select her, or reject her.

'Come, the tea is poured,' said Felicia. 'Miss Dare, you will sit here, and Pedro, you will sit at the other side of me. Tristao, here is your tea in a mug, and you will sit on the step of the fountain and occupy yourself with a strawberry tart and not one of my golden carp. You will also have a tart – Jaine? You will permit me to call you by your first name? It is that you have such a young look, and this is to your advantage, for Tristao has taken to you because of your youthfulness. I think you have been wise in your choice of a *confianca*, Pedro.'

'And why exactly is that, Felicia?' The Duque accepted a cup of tea and lounged back in his seat to enjoy it, and very possibly the picture which the Latin woman made in her soft blue dress seated beneath the table sunshade, little blue gems in the lobes of her ears, like pale shells against the raven gloss of her hair.

'Just wise, *meu caro*. Much more so than in your choice of a – well, let that pass.' Felicia smiled with a Latin sweetness tinged with a touch of irony. 'You have no close family to object to your employment in Brazil – which is a big, strange country for you, Jaine?'

'I lost my parents at a too early age to recall them, and

73

though my aunt was good enough to bring me up I – I have no real bond of closeness with her, or my cousin. We,' Jaine took a sip of tea, 'have such different personalities. They are outgoing people, but I'm a bit of a dreamer, I suppose.'

'Your aunt is going to be surprised when you acquaint her with your news. She is still your legal guardian, I should think.'

'I am twenty-two, *senhora*.' Jaine shot a slightly old-fashioned look at Felicia de Evangel. 'People keep taking me for a teenager, but I've been working as a secretary for the past five years.'

'You really do have an amazing look of youth.' Felicia's eyes flickered over Jaine as she sat there on the white scrolled bench, a finger of sunshine stroking her thin cheek and the side of her neck in the opening of her shirt. The Latin eyes flickered to the Duque, who seemed indolently content to listen without comment, one long leg crossed over the other, his eyes lazy and unreadable. Felicia seemed more than a little curious, as if she would have liked to know exactly how Pedro de Zanto regarded the young woman he was taking into his home; the big house called Goldenhawk that stood between the forest and the sea.

'It is a piquant situation, Pedro,' she said, at last.

'Is it, *cara*?' he drawled.

'You know that it must be, when the *senhorinha* was secretary to her aunt, and that same lady might have become your in-law.' Felicia gave him a very provocative look. 'Are you doing it on purpose? I know what a subtle man you can be, Pedro. And I know, too, that you can sometimes be what your name implies.'

'Hard as stone?' His voice was still sardonic and he showed no sign of being angered by the Senhora's remarks. 'Revengeful, like Pedro the Cruel?'

'It might follow, *meu caro*. More tea?' Felicia held the pot and dared his tawny eyes. He shook his head and

74

glanced at his wristwatch, which was attached to a crocodile band.

'*Gracias,* no. We must be getting back to Miss Dare's hotel. I have a business dinner to attend this evening and time has a way of flying on wings. Tristao, when you have wiped the jam from your fingers you may shake the hand of Jaine in a small good-bye. In a few days we will go home together, but in the meantime be a good boy with your Tia Felicia.'

Tristao looked at his father with that puckish gravity that was beginning to pluck at Jaine's heart. The boy had never known a mother, only these attractive 'aunts' provided by his father, and now a *confianca* provided in place of the mother the boy had expected. None of them could be sure of what was going through the boy's mind, and like the Duque he had thick dark lashes that were a handy concealment for his thoughts. He rose obediently to his feet, held his hands under the fountain, shook them in the sun to dry, and then came to Jaine.

'*Ate a vista, senhorinha,*' he said, and then as he held out a hand to her he seemed to stumble on his weak leg and instantly, her heart turning, Jaine caught hold of him and lightly caressed his cheek with her hand.

'Yes, until we meet again, Tristao.'

They said good-bye to Felicia who came with them to the car while Tristao lingered behind with the cream puffs and the white cat, and perhaps a touch of self-resentment because his leg had revealed its weakness.

There at the side of the grey car the slender, ringed hands of the Latin woman received their due from the lips of the Duque. 'I am more than grateful to you for your care of Tristao,' he said to her. 'You are kind to him even if at times you are rather unkind to me.'

'You can take it, you enigmatical man.' Felicia gave him her slightly mysterious smile, there in the sunlight that brought out the raven lights in her hair. 'To know you even for years is never to know you entirely, Pedro. On one side of the coin you are the most courteous man in the world, but on the other side—' She shrugged her elegant shoulders and glanced into the car at Jaine, who had settled into her seat while the two Latin people bade each other good-bye. Jaine suspected that despite the Senhora's married status she was more provocatively fond of the Duque than she really ought to be, as the wife of the renowned Latin poet Castro de Evangel.

Jaine sat there in a seeming trance of innocence, but she was thinking to herself that Pedro de Zanto was far more devastating than any man had the right to be. He coolly, suavely collected hearts, but Jaine wondered if he had ever truly given his heart to a woman. His well-developed and sensuously tawny body, yes. Beautiful women obviously appealed to his eyes and his senses, but it seemed to Jaine that she was beginning to know a man who was curiously armoured against a deep involvement. Even his break with Laraine had left him with no visible sign of a scar.

'*Adeus*, Miss Dare.' The Senhora de Evangel was gazing in at Jaine with eyes that were inquisitive and yet not unfriendly. Possibly because she saw no rival in Jaine, and because there was some subtle link between her and the Zantos and she cared about the welfare of the child. As a Latin woman she would feel deprived at not having children of her own.

'Thank you for your kindness to me, *senhora*.' Jaine smiled at her and waved good-bye as the car turned smoothly and they drove away from the *quinta*, above which the sun was going pink and adding to the lustre of the rose coloured stone.

It looked a dream house there in the waning sunlight, but Jaine had the feeling that Felicia de Evangel was not married to her dream lover.

They had been driving in silence for some time, in this

76

car whose engine was so quiet only the dashboard clock could be heard ticking, when the Duque suddenly spoke, stirring awake in Jaine that little prickle of nervous awareness. While the car slipped along this ribbon of road with a whisper of silk, she could almost pretend that she was driving along with an intimate friend instead of an intimidating stranger who had decided to take her on to his payroll.

'So that is settled,' he said. 'Even though you won over Tristao with an amusing little trick – and don't imagine I wasn't aware of it – I am quite satisfied that you are right for the job. If I have spurred you a little and made you jib, it was necessary to test your mettle. The wilds of Brazil are as unlike the suburbs of England as you are unlike the women of my country. The countryside around Goldenhawk is wild and exotic and far from picture houses, but as Felicia remarked, you have imagination, and that is a good thing for a *confianca* to have, especially if she is to have charge of a child. You found the Senhora de Evangel a congenial person, eh?'

'Very much so, and extremely nice looking. It is one of the things I like about Latin people—' Jaine broke off and bit her lip, for she was more or less admitting that she found him attractive.

'It is natural for the fair-skinned Angels to find interesting the dark-skinned Latins,' he said, with a quizzical sideglance at Jaíne. 'The charming Felicia has been a friend of Tristao's mother since the boy was born – as I told you, she was a nurse before her marriage.'

'His – mother?' Jaine gasped. 'But I thought – I assumed—'

'That she was dead?'

'Naturally.'

'Why should it be natural? She is a young woman, and childbirth is not automatically fatal.'

'Well, *senhor*, you are still a bachelor—' Jaine floundered, for they had suddenly got into deep waters that almost took

77

her breath away. She hadn't dreamed that Tristao's mother might still be alive ... somehow it had seemed ... Jaine swallowed a dryness from her throat ... somehow she had not wished to believe that Pedro would permit a child of his to be born out of wedlock if he could prevent it.

'Yes, by the grace of a jilting I am still a bachelor,' he drawled. 'Tell me, Miss Dare, are you shocked that a man can be a bachelor and yet have a son? Somehow I assumed that your innocence was of the type that could not be corrupted by the puritan view that a man, and a woman, are doomed to perdition because they surrender to natural inclinations unsanctified at the altar. There can be a love so forceful that it drives out discretion ... just as there can be a physical love that the mind rejects when the sensibilities have taken command again of the senses. It really doesn't always follow, *senhorinha*, that in order to be the parent of the child the man must be the husband of the child's mother. It may sound like a riddle, but there is an answer to it – but that is none of your business.'

As he spoke, and on a savage note that made Jaine feel as if he had lashed out at her with a whip, he swung the car around a cliff bend and there below them the ocean seemed aflame with the burning sun as it dropped out of the day. It was a most beautiful and yet sinister orange sky, and that pagan fire danced its shadows over the Duque's profile and made it seem as if cast in bronze. A hard, striking, unmelting bronze, revealing a man who could be as cruel to a woman as he could be kind to a child.

They drove swiftly beneath the brow of the steep cliffs and the swelling hills where the colour-washed houses crouched, as if their occupants were all too aware of the beauty and the underlying violence of this land steeped in history.

Jaine clenched her fingers together and felt the beating of her dismayed heart. Tristao's mother was still alive, and yet the Duque had thought of putting Laraine Desmond in her place. A riddle, he had said, and it was so subtle and complex a riddle that Jaine felt totally out of her depth when she attempted to solve it.

The only answer possible was that Pedro de Zanto now hated the woman he had once felt an overpowering desire to possess . . . he had put Tristao's mother out of his life but that didn't stop him caring for the boy, to such an extent that he opposed Latin convention and accepted carelessly the label of roué which the affair had attached to him.

Though Jaine was a total innocent when it came to romantic affairs, she could never be shocked by the Duque's flagrant love of his own flesh and blood. What did shock her was that he seemed so careless of his own personal happiness (he must have known that a self-devoted beauty such as Laraine could never make him truly happy) and so savagely unforgiving when it came to the woman who had borne Tristao. He was deep . . . deep as that dark sea down there, and to love him was to fall into those depths and not know how or when your heart would be broken.

'Well, are we now up against some prudish doubts regarding your position in my household?' The words sprang at her in the growing darkness, as if to savage her feelings that had never been aroused or tested by an overwhelming desire. 'Has Tristao fallen from grace because he came into the world a love child instead of a matrimonial blessing?'

'No.' Jaine spoke with angry pain in her voice, that he should lash at her and accuse her of prudery. 'You have no right to speak to me like that—'

'I have the right of an employer who sees gilt where he believed he caught a glimpse of gold. All was rather romantically tragic while you believed Tristao's mother to be dead, but now you learn that she is very much alive you mount your virginal high horse and flourish the whip of virtue.'

'It's you who are lashing out at me,' she protested. 'It seemed natural enough to suppose that your – that Tristao's

79

mother had died, and I'd be wholly contemptuous of myself if I turned against a child for any reason. I – I like your son very much, *senhor*, and I am more than ever certain that I want to be his companion.'

'Then why are we quarrelling?' he said sardonically, as he switched on the roof light and it revealed the strained whiteness of Jaine's face. 'The job is yours, Miss Dare, and I lay down only one hard and fast rule – you will refrain from being curious about the boy's mother. You will ask no questions about her, and will in fact continue to think of her as having gone out of this life.'

'Very well, *senhor*.' Jaine's fingers relaxed their tense hold on each other, and she could feel the pain as they unclasped. 'I expect you will want me to apply for a permit to work in Brazil?'

'No, that will not be necessary.' He spoke curtly. 'As far as the authorities are concerned you are an English guest in my house, and if I pay you money to take care of Tristao that is no one's business but mine.'

'But, *senhor*, I don't understand. I think I should apply for the correct permit.' Jaine gave him a bewildered look. 'You will be employing me, for the authorities already know that I came into the country with very little money.'

'I am the Duque Almanzor de Ros Zanto, and even in Brazil a man in my position is allowed a certain freedom. I don't wish you to approach the authorities over this matter of coming to stay at Goldenhawk. It is enough that you are my guest – or are you afraid that people will take you for my mistress?'

Jaine flushed at the cruel sting to his question, and if it hadn't been for the haunting little image of Tristao that she carried in her mind she would have told the Duque to go to the devil. He was hell to love, and though she had never hoped for heaven, she knew what a fool she was to endure this kind of torture,

'Say it,' he drawled. 'Call me a devil and be done with it.'

'Y-you are a devil,' she said tensely. 'Y-your only saving grace is that you love Tristao, and if it wasn't for that I wouldn't come within a mile of Goldenhawk.'

The flash of his teeth was fierce as she said those words, and Jaine sensed that never before in his autocratic life had a mere employee spoken to him with such freedom. But as the car sped on towards the lights of Porto de Zanto, Jaine couldn't help but wonder what his behaviour would be like once she entered his domain and found herself cut off from contact with her only relatives, far away in England. She felt sure that Madge would never forgive her ... she would regard it as a blatant betrayal that Jaine chose to work for the very man whom Laraine had lost the courage to marry.

Madge might even suppose that Jaine was pursuing him herself ... a thought that drove the colour into Jaine's cheeks and made her bite her lip quite painfully.

It couldn't be true, could it? Was she obeying an impulse of the heart that involved the Duque far more potently than it involved the boy? Was she allowing his dark and subtle attraction to overrule her good sense?

The car slid smoothly to a halt in front of the hotel where she was staying. 'Jaine.' The Duque spoke her name almost with menace. 'Tristao is not to be disappointed a second time, and if you do a moonlight flit in the way of your cousin I shall, this time, be very angry indeed. When I am angry I can make life intolerable for the person responsible for my loss of good will – do you understand me?'

'I think so,' she said quietly. 'You can pick up the telephone and make a complaint about me which can be relayed to the plane so that I am not allowed to leave when it lands. As you have such a great deal of authority I wonder you allowed Laraine to slip out of your clutches. She had so much more to offer than I have.'

81

'You mean she would have been my bride?' The overhead light gleamed down on his face and showed the ironical tilt to his left eyebrow. 'I believe you are a very romantic creature, Miss Dare, who would like to believe that two people marry for the single reason that they are madly in love. Marriage without this would seem a blasphemy to you, eh?'

'I think it would, *senhor*.' Her hand sought the projection that opened the door beside her, but just as she would have released herself from the car, the Duque reached across her slim body and secured her hand with his, the action bringing him so darkly close to Jaine that she almost gave way to panic and struggled with him. His eyes locked with hers, holding her mesmerized only a moment after that flash of primitive fear ran through her body.

'Please,' she murmured, 'I have to go in. I'm weary, for I've been out all day—'

'Yes,' he agreed, 'a little weary, a lot worried, and still afraid to live your own life. Afraid of that, and yet unhesitant to dare the wheels of my car. You are something of an enigma, Jaine Dare. If I were a kinder man I might let you return to your uncongenial life in the belief that there is less danger for you there even if there is less excitement. But I am not altogether a kind man. My motive might even be one of Latin revenge, as Felicia intimated. Taking you from your aunt as secretary, removing you from the orbit of Laraine who needs someone to pick up the broken pieces of her discarded toys. Whatever will they do without you, Jaine?'

'I – I expect they'll manage.' Jaine felt herself trapped in her seat by him, held captive by his tawny eyes, and close as never before to the hard danger of his ruthless male body. His dominance had hold of her heart as well as her body and filled with a sudden fear that he would see this in her eyes, Jaine lowered her lashes and allowed her eyelids to droop tiredly over her eyes.

'May I go now, *senhor*? It has been a long day, and you have a business meeting, haven't you?'

'I have,' he drawled. 'Yes, you droop like an English flower which has been exposed to a little too much tropic sunlight. It is a white flower I am thinking of, Virgin's Ladder, or some such name, with dense green leaves which likes the shade of trees. Anyway, be off with you, Jaine, and have ready your belongings by the day after tomorrow. Pay your hotel bill tomorrow – here is the money.'

He let go of her and took from the inside pocket of his coat a leather wallet. This time Jaine drew blood as she bit her lip. She had of necessity to accept the money and it would have been easier to do so had he not been so adamant that she not apply for a working permit to stay in Brazil. His attitude was a bit of a mystery, but he was just not a man to be defied – or denied. He took her hand again and tucked some bills into her palm.

'A car will call for you between eight and nine o'clock of Thursday morning. Be ready, *senhorinha*. It will take you to the airstrip just beyond the town and with Tristao and myself you will fly to Goldenhawk.'

Her fingers clenched around the notes he had given her. 'Is it – that far?' she asked, and this time she couldn't keep the tremor out of her voice.

'It is where the ocean meets the Amazon; where the forest meets the jungle.' As he spoke he stepped from the car and with a courtesy that was suddenly a little aloof he escorted Jaine to the swing doors of the hotel.

'*Boa noite*, Jaine.' He bent over her hand but he didn't salute it with his lips, as he had saluted the hand of Felicia de Evangel. He gave her a brief, enigmatical smile, and as she slipped through the swing doors Pedro returned to his car. The headlamps swooped in an arc as she turned to look, and with silken smoothness the big car drove away into the night.

CHAPTER SIX

IT seemed incredible that such luxury should be cruising so silently through the sky. The body of the private plane did not hold seats at either side of the central aisle; it was a high-speed travelling lounge, with sofas, a carpet covering the floor, and music relayed softly from a polished radio. On a low table in front of the sofas the contents of a picnic-case had been spread, cold chicken, buttered rolls, fruit and a golden wine poured into chiselled glasses.

Tristao sat reading a comic book, in his hand a milk drink flavoured deliciously with strawberries. Jaine had rather fancied the drink, but when the Duque poured wine for two she didn't like to refuse it. It would have sounded so silly and young to say that this trip was enough to make her intoxicated.

From the window nearby she gazed down at the jungle above which they were flying, rich green land ribboned by deep water, the surface of which had the sheen of molten metal. Now and then they flew among luminous clouds, when nothing could be seen and only the breath of a strange seduction could be felt. Everything she had known so well was being left behind and the private aircraft of Pedro de Zanto was carrying her on swift wings to a new life that fluttered tiny wings inside her.

Left behind, also, in the wastepaper basket of her hotel room was the wire she had received that morning from Madge Desmond. It ordered her to return home and stated explicitly that if she didn't do so, then Madge would have nothing more to do with her. After reading the wire Jaine had felt a sense of guilt and had paced her balcony wondering anew if she was doing the right thing. For a while she had felt so indecisive that she had felt a certain sympathy

84

with people who had to consult gipsy fortune-tellers and astrology charts before they made a momentous decision that would change the course of their life.

As the wire had slowly crumpled in her nervous hand, Jaine had contrasted the old life with the possible new; the dominance of a man in place of the selfish demands of her aunt: the anger of the Duque if she let him down at the very last moment.

Now, seated in his private plane, the blue smoke from a rare cigar drifting across her nose, she could no longer tell if fear or favour had made up her mind for her. All she was certain of was that she was here, feeling the smooth motion of the plane, and the taste of wine on her lips.

Tristao had made the trip before and so he could lose himself in the adventures of Superman, but Jaine, though never for a single moment unaware of the Duque, was fascinated by the journey. She had eaten very little breakfast and could only peck at the chicken salad, for that world below her seemed so strange and forbidding as the clouds parted to reveal it, and so deceptively beautiful where the rivers ran like ribbons of sun-melted silver.

'Beside those rivers,' said the Duque, leaning forward to watch *his* world with her, 'the great black crocodiles lie in the sun-baked mud. They have eyes like golden nuggets buried in layers of rock, a most primitive beast, with none of the beauty to be found in most creatures of the forest. A cruel beast as well.'

'Is not the puma cruel, and the eagle?' she asked, not daring to turn her head in case she looked into those tawny eyes that quickened all the dangers and excitements of this new life she was daring to make for herself.

'They are cruel only when they are hungry or hurt,' he said, a curl of his blue smoke flying softly against her cheek, close to her small ear against the smoothness of her hair. 'Don't you know that primitive things have less cruelty in them than the harassed creatures on a city street? The worst kind of injury is inflicted by people so absorbed in themselves that they spare not a glance of pity for another's pain of body or torment of soul. Ambition drives them; its tyranny blinds them to the fact that others have nerves to be torn, senses to be bruised ... you would be less than the intelligent young person I take you for if you did not guess that my country is torn in two by ambitious bigots.'

'I had heard,' she murmured, nostrils tensed to his cigar smoke; her nerves tensed to his nearness. 'I did rather feel that you were not in sympathy with certain of your country's policies.'

'Bear that in mind, Jaine, if at any time my mood has teeth in it and you feel I might bite.' His voice became quizzical. 'There are Mayan Indians at my house who work for me, but don't let them frighten you. In time you will grow accustomed to them and make friends with them. At first they will be a little suspicious of you, for they are a pure-bred people I have never allowed to become citified. They belong to this part of the world and would only be spoiled by city life. Handsome, graceful, and loyal, the true descendants of the Mayas who were here when the first caravels came from the old world to explore, and plunder, of course. As a girl fond of books you are no doubt good at history?'

'Quite good,' she said. 'Some of your ancestors were extremely ruthless, *senhor.*'

'I admit it,' he drawled. 'But the *conquistadores* did not have it all their own way. Have you not heard of the Don Pedro who was forced by the Mayas to drink boiling gold? What a supreme piece of judgment meted out to a golden pirate!'

Jaine gave a shiver at the picture evoked of Indian justice to a man who ransacked and ravished in order to fill the gold vaults of Portugal. She glanced at the golden wine on the sofa table, and she heard the Duque laugh softly.

'You have a vivid imagination, Jaine. What a pity that for so long it has been locked up and kept out of sight like a

86

family secret. Come, drink your wine and learn to like your freedom.'

'Am I really free?' she asked, and this time she looked at him, into those eyes with the carved eyelids, so pagan in their beauty, so worldly in their regard of her youthful unsophistication. 'When I look upon your world, *senhor*, it seems to me like an intricate cage enclosed by the mountains and the sea. It frightens me a little.'

'What frightens you is your own temerity in daring to fly from your aunt's cage into the sunlight. I know that divided loyalties can be hell, and that duty has a stern voice. But you have paid back your family debt well above the mark, and neither Madge Desmond nor her daughter are helpless creatures. Forget them, Jaine!'

'Is that an order, *senhor*?'

'If you like.'

'You say it with such careless arrogance, as if Laraine never meant anything to you. Yet she must have done—'

'Must?' He blew a careless ring of smoke. 'My dear child, because your cousin is beautiful and worth, perhaps, adding to a man's collection of possessions, you must not suppose that she is automatically gifted with the rare virtue of being able to make a man forget all other women ... a virtue known as love, I believe. Life has made a cynic of me, but even I have reason to believe that just once in a lifetime this rare creature may cross a man's path and with only a glance steal the heart he had thought so safe behind the iron bars of his disillusion.'

'Then it can't make you feel very proud that you were going to make a mere possession of Laraine.'

'How prim and proper you sound, Jaine, as if you would like to rap me over the knuckles with your ruler.' There was an amused, unrepentant note in his voice. 'I am convinced that your cousin's greatest ambition is to be the most prized possession in a rich man's art collection. She really doesn't wish to be loved, Jaine, for love brings a woman down off

87

her pedestal. And I, quite frankly, had no love in mind when I proposed to her. At that time she suited me. She no longer suits me. It is as simple as that. She most gratified me at the moment she released me.'

'And if she had not,' Jaine looked at him with shocked eyes, 'you would have gone through with a – a loveless marriage?'

'I imagine so, Jaine.' His eyes were wickedly intent upon the look on Jaine's face. 'And because I am grateful to Laraine for sending an emissary to set me free, I have returned to her the diamond jewellery which suited her so well. I am sure it will help sweeten the blow of your desertion from the Desmond menage. According to popular belief, diamonds are a girl's best friend, are they not?'

'You, *senhor*, are a terrible cynic!'

'And beyond redemption, *senhorinha*?'

'Don't ask me that,' Jaine rejoined. 'I don't know the extent of your sins.'

'Or, perhaps, the extent of my virtues?'

'True,' she admitted, and couldn't help a little glance at Tristao. A man in the Duque's position could have had the boy cared for incognito, but he had chosen to declare openly his parenthood and he had Tristao with him as often as possible. He was a surprisingly good father, even if less gentlemanly when it came to the women in his life.

'You, of course, have nothing but your virtue,' he mocked quietly. 'And being such a quaint little saint you feel you have the right to take to task a man who seems a veritable satan in your eyes. This trip to Goldenhawk must seem the most dangerous journey of your life, Jaine.'

'I do keep wondering what would happen if we crashed among hostile Indians,' she said smartly.

His lip arched in that silent laugh and he reached to an ashtray to stub the end of his cigar. 'You can depend upon my pilot even if you are unsure if you can depend upon me. Do you see the job ahead of you as a kind of vocation? Do you plan to try and make a better man of me?'

'I thought my task was to be Tristao's *confianca*, not your confessor,' she rejoined. 'You seem to find me an easy target for your mockery, *senhor*. I might well ask if you plan to make me your court jester?'

At once the expression of his face underwent a subtle, almost dangerous alteration. The bold lips straightened into a stern line, and the tawny eyes looked hard and cold. 'Be careful,' he said, with a menacing softness, 'that you don't make me angry with you. It is one thing for me to be cynical, but I don't care to hear it on your lips. Funnily enough, *menina*, I am worldly enough to admire a girl of virtue, for virtue has the rarity of a blue diamond these days. It is for that in you that I want you in contact with Tristao. I had no idea before our meeting that such as yourself could be provided for the boy. Companion, playmate, teacher, even at times a bit of a nurse.'

The Duque sat back in his seat frowning at her, an image of annoyed distinction in his pearl-grey suit and wine-coloured shirt, his pale tie impeccable against the wine silk. '*Por deus*, I should not be angry. Along with all that you are but a schoolgirl! Untutored by life. Unused to any velvet-glove treatment. It would be strange if you were not suspicious of me.' Abruptly he smiled, his fine teeth glimmering against his firm, dark-gold skin. 'When half a saint meets half a satan there is bound to be sulphur in the air. You agree?'

'Yes.' Her smile was tentative as she turned back to the window, where far below the jungle seemed less savage than that glimpse of temper in the Duque. A shiver ran the length of her spine. 'Have we much further to go?'

'As the hawk flies,' he drawled. 'Tristao, *meu caro*, you seem mightily absorbed in that comic book. I am not sure that I should let you read that kind of absurdity.'

'It is not absurd, Papa.' As Tristao spoke Jaine glanced round and saw the father and son looking solemnly at each other. 'I am reading all about Tarzan who lived also in the jungle. He was most interesting and could speak the language of all the animals. He was really a nobleman, like you, Papa.'

In an instant the Duque's smile took on such an indulgent quality that Jaine all but caught her breath. He really was a marvellous man when it came to his son. One caught sight of that nobility bred in his bones, and in those of the child. One saw culture allied to an unconventional spirit no one had truly tamed.

'If I recall the good Tarzan had a tendency to swing through the trees. You will not emulate him in that, *chico*, even if our Miss Dare can teach you to purr like a cat.'

Tristao grinned and looked at Jaine. 'Tarzan has a wife called Jane,' he said. 'They have a house in the jungle built into the trees, but much smaller than Goldenhawk, of course. I bet you have never seen a house like ours, *senhorinha*. It has all sorts of hiding places, and a tower, though I wish there were not so many twisting stairs, for they make my leg ache, except when Papa carries me up on his shoulders.' At mention of his leg a frown linked the boy's fine eyebrows together and he bent again over his book. There was a little silence, and when Jaine stole a look at the Duque she saw that he was suddenly lost in his thoughts, which were obviously connected with Tristao's lameness. There seemed no doubt that every attempt had been made to completely heal the leg, but the injury suffered when he was a mere infant had been sufficiently severe to leave him with a permanent handicap. As he grew older it would not be possible for him to become involved in sports, though Jaine didn't doubt that he could swim, and also ride. He would always be slightly crippled, and for a man as superbly well made as the Duque this would seem a shame. He would want Tristao to be as much like himself as possible ... though Jaine, who thought the boy adorable, could never imagine him quite so striking in appearance as his father.

His features were not so regular and did not show a promise of dominance. His gaze had a fey quality and Jaine did not feel that his eyes would ever be as wickedly sensuous as the Duque's. The boy would grow up to be lean and attractive, she was certain of that, but he would never possess the subtle and pervasive power of his father; that ruthless ability of a man who liked his own way and had the will to get it. All that was romantic and gentle in the nature of Pedro de Zanto had probably been passed on to the child, and as if the Duque saw the better part of him reflected in the boy, he loved him and cared for him as he seemed unwilling to care for the mother.

Jaine couldn't help but feel curious about the woman who had loved Pedro and borne this sensitive and intelligent child because of that love. And though she had been warned to keep her curiosity to herself, she would have been less than human not to feel a greed to know if the girl had been lovely, and why the desire had turned to disenchantment.

And then, as if afraid that curiosity might be seen in her eyes if the Duque was to look at her in that sudden way of his, Jaine returned her attention to the view beyond the windows of the private plane. Airborne, she thought bemusedly. On her way to the house with the fascinating name, which had hideaways and a tower. A smile stirred on her lips. For her this was a momentous journey; a flight from the past into a future that was bound to hold elements of delight and terror.

Suddenly below the plane the dense velvety masses of foliage had given way to the spreading acres of *terra roxa*, the purple earth in which the coffee flourished. Jaine caught her breath at the pulse-stirring view. There they were, the coffee-terraced hills with their flame-brown look, among which the coffee workers would be busy, wide straw hats shading them from the hot sun. And now she saw vivid patches of green-gold, which she knew to be the sugar-cane which grew alongside the coffee hills.

Her heart seemed to open to the wild beauty stretched below her eager gaze; to open and then close to keep intact the image of the cultivated lands of the Duque Pedro Almanzor de Ros Zanto, whose background was linked to a vivid, cruel, yet in some ways splendid history. Though ruthless those seekers of a new world had been incredibly brave and daring. In her own veins ran the Huguenot history and she couldn't help but respond to all that was wild and free, and to wonder what battles lay in store between her and the man who held the whip hand over a jungle that fought day and night to overrun the terraced coffee trees and the tall spears of golden sugar-cane.

He would delight in such a battle, she thought. He was a ruthless man, and yet she prized his esteem ... very highly.

As she leaned to the window the nape of her neck seemed to prickle and she knew instantly that the Duque was looking at her. 'We are over the coffee terraces, *sim*?'

'Yes, *senhor*. They are a fabulous sight.'

'I am glad you approve. Soon we will be coming in sight of the landing stretch, so please to sit back in your seat and fasten your belt.' He rose as he spoke and saw to the belt around Tristao. Then he sat down again and shot a brief smile at Jaine. 'You are looking just a trifle fraught. Are you nervous of the landing, or has it suddenly hit you that right now you are a long way from home?'

'I am a long way from England,' she said, and could feel the tiny nerves pulling at her lips. 'Half a world away, and I must admit that I'm very unsure of my very new wings.'

'In a few days you will feel more confident. I had not thought to ask before, but have you belongings which you would like to have dispatched from England to Goldenhawk? It can be arranged.'

Jaine thought of her rather plain room just off the bathroom at Madge's flat. Half the size of Laraine's, and furnished out with orphan chairs and worn carpets from the other rooms. In the wardrobe hung a few dresses and a winter coat. On the bookshelf reclined a few books, for on her wages Jaine couldn't afford to buy books and so she borrowed them from the Westminster Library. In the drawers of the dressing-table were a few more bits and pieces, but most of what she owned was in the suitcase she had brought to Brazil.

It shocked her that she owned so little, and her lashes screened her eyes as she replied that she had lived with her aunt and therefore had no real belongings of her own.

She heard the click as the Duque fastened his seat-belt. That sharp click was the only comment he made, yet very strangely it almost brought tears to Jaine's eyes. For an instant she had felt as if he reached out in brusque sympathy to her . . . a man who had never known what it felt like to be denied whatever took his fancy.

Half an hour later, seated in the back seat of a fast-moving jeep with Tristao beside her, the excitement of the flight still tingled in Jaine's veins, along with the wondrous shock of having felt a man such as the Duque in sympathy with a girl like herself. Of course, he could have been pitying her for a deprived person, but Jaine believed he had been profoundly startled that someone should possess only what fitted into a medium-sized suitcase. While he . . . he owned all this, and more!

The Duque drove the jeep, as if he needed the activity after the fairly long flight, and as they sped along Tristao pointed to this and that, all of which flew by in a dreamlike way, an unreal vista of a rugged shoreline leading to Goldenhawk.

She heard the changing of the gears as the jeep began to climb uphill, and the cliffs at their side took on an almost menacing steepness, towering above the narrow frills of sand at the foot of them, edged by uneven lacings of white foam. Bat-shaped, rubbery plants brushed their wheels, and from some of the trees hung leaves as long as a man, curving like great sickles in the sun. As they mounted higher the foliage became denser, until suddenly split apart by stone walls and those immense gate-posts that always seemed to mark the driveways of Latin property.

Birds called but could not be seen in the density of trees crowding the driveway, which snaked among them like a shadowy tunnel, so that she and Tristao smiled at each other and held hands as the jeep thrust forward into the dappled gloom, almost like a snakeskin of dark green and gold.

Jaine's heart was beating with excitement, for soon ... soon now the gloom would lift and she would have come home to Goldenhawk. She, and not Laraine, whom she had faintly envied that day on the hotel balcony, before she had learned from Madge that the wedding was off.

Her eyes dwelt on the wide shoulders and the dark proud head of the man seated at the wheel in front of her. What were his thoughts at this precise moment? Was he at all regretful that instead of bringing home a bride he merely brought home a *confianca* for his son?

The snaking drive took a sudden turn to the left and Jaine caught her breath as the jeep ran beneath an immense archway and entered the courtyard of the house that stood with the sea below it and with the jungle at its boundaries. Their wheels bumped over the square cobbling that must have been as old as the magnificent pair of *ceiba* trees that held at bay some of the brilliant sunlight with branches strong and ancient as the Indian legends.

Above the courtyard and reached by steps at either side of the house was a flagstone terrace jutting out on stone pillars and beneath this were the cool Manoeline cloisters so loved by all Latins, with fantastic traceries of stone and iron, and there at the centre a bronze hawk, its sharp beak in the air and immense wings outspread in petrified flight.

Goldenhawk, chiselled out of tawny-gold stone, rich with a velvety patchwork of vines, perched in all its drama on a wide sweeping plateau of land.

Jaine climbed from the jeep in something of a daze, for though she had expected a certain old-world grandeur, she had not realized that the place would grab at her imagination and crowd it in an instant with images of the *conquistadore* who had built it, and his fine lady who had travelled by sea to be mistress of the house . . . wearing one of those jewelled poison-rings as protection of her honour should pirates board the ship.

Down the years this house had welcomed many women, but it seemed to Jaine that never before had it opened its richly carved doors to someone as insignificant as herself, clad not in silk and fine footwear but in a cartwheel hat of woven straw, and an orange shirt over pale-coloured slacks, with sandals on her feet.

So many windows indicating the rambling range of rooms, each window protected by carved wooden shutters. And huge terracotta pots set at different levels and overflowing with brilliant flowers. Huge tropical flowers that mingled their colours with the poinsettias like suspended scarlet candelabra, the sandalwood pink of hibiscus, and a vine of a dazzling tangerine hue, where hummingbirds hung like spinning tops and stabbed their beaks into the honeyed hearts of the trumpets. Loveliest of all was the jacaranda tree, which was supposed to be the symbol of love and poetry.

Jaine gazed at the profuse mauve flowers and wondered which Zanto bride had planted jacaranda here at Goldenhawk . . . a shimmering bride of a tree among these jungle exotics.

A shadow fell at Jaine's side, joining hers on the cobbles. '*Gosta de estar aqui senhorinha?*'

'*Sim, gosta muito, senhor,*' she replied in his language. She glanced up at the Duque and had no idea that her green eyes took on a mysterious quality beneath the brim of her straw hat. 'How could anyone with a scrap of imagination

95

not like Goldenhawk?'

'How indeed, but it has been known,' he said enigmatically. 'But I don't think I had many doubts about your reaction. A lonely spirit reaches out to a lonely house, and as you see our nearest neighbours are the ocean and the jungle.'

'So many flowers,' she murmured. 'Cultivated from the wild jungle variety, I can see that. Orchids, gardenias and roses that would cost a small fortune in a London flower shop. It's amazing!'

'Have an orchid for nothing.' He reached up an arm and plucked one from the branch of a palm tree, where a spray of the lovely strange things had taken root. He handed the orchid to Jaine, who gazed in wonder at the purple-brown petals spattered with the sheerest drops of gold. The petals felt like velvet to the touch, but the orchid had no scent, as if to protect its beauty from the bees and the hummingbirds. Jaine cradled the orchid in her hands as she walked with the Duque and his son across the courtyard to the Manoeline cloisters which evidently gave access to the house. Pedro would never know that she meant to press the orchid into her diary and to keep it always, a memento of her arrival at Goldenhawk, and a reminder, if she needed one, that for now and always he had her heart and that in her heart she was as beautiful as the flower.

Shade fell around them as they stepped beneath the carved stone of the cloisters, above which the bronze hawk guarded the armorial crest of the family, and suddenly silent-footed servants in white livery appeared, bowing to the Duque and then to Tristao, but passing Jaine by as if she were not there. Two of them were going to the jeep to collect the luggage but the third, who was a brown-gold colour with the face of an Inca warrior, remained to address words to the Duque and to take his orders.

They did not speak in Portuguese until abruptly the Duque turned to Jaine and introduced her to his distinctive manservant. 'Jaine, this is Primitivo, who runs the house on wheels of oil, and who will always ensure that you have all you need. Way back in his ancestry there is Maya nobility, as you can see, and he came into this household as an infant of two, when his mother was savaged by a puma, which my father had to shoot. As boys Primitivo and I used to shoot the jungle rapids on a gracefully built *baleau*, and it was exhilarating dropping from one water level to the next in that flimsy punt. You have in your hand a pretty enough orchid, but Primitivo knows where to find the huge white orchid, the Cristata, as it is called. My Indians look fierce, but they have kind hearts, and at first they will treat you as if you are non-existent. It is just their way with regard to women – you understand?'

'I am sure I understand.' Jaine gave the tall, grave-faced Indian a smile, to which his only response was a faint softening of the amazingly dark eyes, set at a sloping angle in his strong-boned face, and lustrous as black satin. He looked at Tristao, and then glanced back at her, and Jaine could only suppose that he thought her very young to be the *senhorito's confianca*.

The Duque spoke to him again in the language Jaine couldn't yet hope to understand, and then he went silently away into the deeper regions of the house.

The Duque opened a glass-framed door leading into a salon, and with the traditional words he invited Jaine to enter. 'Be welcome and regard my house as yours.'

'Thank you,' she murmured, and stepped into a most beautiful room panelled with golden-flecked walls and with creamy alpaca rugs scattered upon the dark timber of the floor, which around the silky wool rugs was polished to a deep gloss. There were several pieces of carved furniture of the colonial era, dark and splendid, with touches of gold. Silver plate and treasured porcelain made pools of light and colour against the rich patina of the woods, and here and there on the walls were knights and madonnas in solid golden frames.

Jaine would have thought the room beautifully formal had it not been for a great couch upholstered in tawny jaguar hides, with set in front of it a long coffee-table of gleaming jungle wood. Upon the table stood a carved box that probably contained cigars, and above the couch upon the wall was a framed feather picture of an Aztec noble, wearing a cloak of iridescent feathers and a golden bird headdress.

'That is very old,' said the Duque, coming to her side and studying the picture with her. 'Such artistry was the work of the nuns at the Wailing Dove convent, and I think you can guess how that picture came into my family. Exquisite workmanship, revealing a depth of patience we of this age have no conception of. Each tiny feather like a piece of embroidery, and exact in detail. All that is left of an old love story.'

Jaine side-glanced at the Duque's profile and saw not irony but a certain indulgence stamped upon it. Was he thinking that he had been luckier . . . he had a living memento of his love affair in contrast to a feather painting sent to that other Duque Pedro by the girl he loved who had taken the veil.

Was it possible . . . Jaine's pulses gave a throb. Was it remotely on the cards that the mother of Tristao had also taken the veil? Had Pedro not said that in his family the pagan and the pure were curiously interwoven? Had he not implied that Zanto history had a way of repeating itself?

His eyes found hers with that disconcerting suddenness, before she could look away and conceal her thoughts. He stared into her eyes, and then his brows drove together into that black and rather forbidding line. His eyes raked over her face as if he scorned her virtuous curiosity about him and the woman to whom he had made passionate love. Colour filtered into Jaine's cheeks, whose high bones gave to her face the shape of a heart. The tormented look of the shy and the unwanted came into her eyes; a certain look of pleading that he not be angry because she was young enough, and romantic enough, to like happy endings to love stories.

A strange little duel of tension seemed to go on between them, broken as all at once a great tall dog bounded into the room and made straight for the Duque. A handsome wolfhound, the fabled companion of noble men, who thrust its head and ears into the Duque's grasp, and gave a whine of pleasure that the master was home again.

'Meet Arno,' said the Duque, and reaching out abruptly for Jaine's hand he forced her to caress the animal's head. 'Show him from the start that you are unafraid and he will be your friend. Arno is like me. He takes to those who dare his bite.'

In that moment, as it happened, Jaine was more nervous of the master than the dog, and quite daringly she ran her fingers over the rough curly coat. '*Como esta*, Arno? You are quite a noble rogue, aren't you? With a jaw big enough to bite my head off.'

'The *senhorinha* likes you, Arno.' Tristao stood patting the wolfhound, who after taking a look at Jaine had turned his attention to the tall figure in pearl-grey, on whom the animal's eyes were fixed as upon an idol.

'Later on,' the Duque promised him. 'We will take our walk when all is settled with the new member of our ménage. Come, Tristao! Come, Jaine! We will go and see if all is well with your apartment. You will both want to rest after that long journey.'

They crossed the hall, with Arno ambling along behind them, and mounted a handsome oval staircase with wrought-iron inset beneath the polished handrail.

'I am here,' Jaine thought in wonderment. And it was like walking a forbidden path, in another girl's footprints, to face a destiny not truly hers.

CHAPTER SEVEN

THE air was coolly stirred by the blades of the fan turning with regularity in the ceiling. The batwing shadows played again and again over the ivory walls of the room, and Jaine watched them lazily from the cushioned divan where she rested and was clad comfortably in a pale green robe.

She could be at ease, for she had seen Tristao off to sleep in his bedroom, with its set of carved fruitwood furniture, deep toy cupboard, and a balcony enclosed in a *mirador*, as was her own balcony, this suite of rooms being at the rear of the house overlooking the delightful discovery of a bathing pool lined with lovely glazed tiles which had not lost their lustre down the years.

As the fan revolved with a cool purring sound, Jaine reflected that Goldenhawk was a fascinating mixture of the old and the fairly new. The *miradors* were most certainly a left-over from the past, where the ladies of the household would have watched male visitors to the house from behind the intricate latticework of the balcony enclosures, indolently fluttering a fan as the dark eyes studied the men and liked or disliked their voices and their features.

The days of secrecy and intrigue, thought Jaine, her bare feet curling together as she let her own eyes travel once again around this large, high-ceilinged room with its cream and gold rococo work, the ivory panels of the walls outlined in gilded patterns. Within the panels were vividly painted, prancing gold horses and their silver-armoured riders. A recessed corner of the room was taken up by a carved and gilded relic cupboard, a veritable dovecote of tiny, glass-fronted shelves adorned with a collection of small porcelain objects. They added a feminine charm to the room, which was otherwise furnished with great cupboards rising to the ceiling, and with a colonial bed covered in ivory lace, whose four tall posts were dark and polished and carved from top to bottom into figures and foliage and satyr faces peering among the carved leaves.

The divan where Jaine lay was placed within the circular alcove of the window that widened out into the lattice-enclosed balcony. And beyond a door at the far end of the room was her very own bathroom, which was also circular and contained a sunken tub completely lined with rose-pink *azulejos*, those silken smooth and lovely tiles so traditional in the house of a Latin and a symbol of the joy of life at the root of their outward dignity and hint of introspection. The faucets of the bath were of rose quartz, and upon variegated shelves of the same lovely quartz stood flagons of bath-crystals and delicate dusting powder. Jaine had sniffed their expensive perfume, and inevitably she had wondered if this apartment had been meant for Laraine.

Then Jaine had laughed a little at her own fantastic innocence. The bedroom did not communicate with the master-bedroom, and even if the Duque had implied that he was marrying for convenience, it would hardly mean that he meant to be a father figure to his bride and not a real husband. He would be that all right, even if love in the truest sense did not enter into the arrangement. In the first place he was a Latin and reared to the arranged-marriage tradition; in the second place he was very much a man and unlikely to ignore a beautiful bride.

Jaine stared at her toes, which unlike her cousin's were unpainted to match her fingernails. Gilding the lily was one thing, but Jaine had never dared to try and gild her own person. A plain book looked best in a plain wrapper, like the slim green diary on the low table at her side. In the entry for this momentous day all she had written was that she had arrived safely at Goldenhawk and hoped to like it there and hoped to be accepted as a useful member of the household.

Even in her diary Jaine could not reveal her inner self; the self that was too cloistered, too afraid that someone might see what she wrote and scoff at the idea of plain Jaine Dare falling in love with any man, let alone a man of lofty birth, much wealth, and such devilish charisma that he probably had women in love with him from one end of the Latin world to the other.

Jaine could not have written of her love had she been tied to a stake and set alight. She could not have borne the mortification of anyone knowing that she cared for Pedro de Zanto, for they would regard it as a joke; the forlorn hope of a girl destined to be unloved.

The strange and lovely orchid was all that bore witness to her love ... she had pressed it between the pages of the diary before the gold-flecked petals could wilt. No one was to know that *he* had plucked it for her. By now the Duque himself would have forgotten the gesture meant only as a courtesy on his side, unaware that for Jaine it had been a deep delight to be handed a flower by him. It was a new experience, something to be remembered and recorded without any words to betray her ... in any case words could not express her mixture of joy and terror at finding herself at Goldenhawk. She knew only that when this day was long over, she would need only to open her diary and the faded flower would be fresh again and she would be wafted back to a courtyard in the sun, where the humming-birds were a whirling mist of colour, and where she felt at home as she had never been in the house of her own relations.

Immersed in her thoughts, Jaine gave a slight jump as the bedroom door abruptly opened and her heart hammered as she saw the tall object of her thoughts enter the room, clad in narrow dark trousers and a polo shirt that was very white against the warm darkness of his skin.

'I did knock,' he said, 'but you must have been napping. I have been out with Arno, and now I feel in need of some coffee and thought to have it here with you, if you don't mind?'

Jaine could only shake her head, for it left her speechless that the Duque should appear in her bedroom at the moment her thoughts had been full of him. Again she was aware of how unconventional he was for a Latin, for quite casually he hooked a chair to the side of her divan and sat down in it. 'Tristao is in dreamland.' His white teeth glimmered as he took note of Jaine's ruffled hair and green robe. 'The coffee will be brought to us in a few minutes; it is coffee grown on the estate and I think you will enjoy it.'

'I – I'm sure I shall, *senhor*.' Jaine felt that she ought to swing her legs to the floor and not loll like this among cushions, not in his presence, but even as she moved he put out a hand and pressed her back against the big ivory-coloured cushions. His hand felt warm and strong through the thin stuff of her robe, and his touch, impersonal though it was, shook Jaine to the core.

'Don't be disturbed because I am here,' he said dryly. 'I wanted to find out if you were feeling settled. You like this apartment, Jaine?'

'Very much, *senhor*.' She could tell from his eyes that he knew that never in her life before had she been into such a room, let alone slept in a colonial bed, surrounded by antique furniture, with a wonderful carpet of Kashan tigers and paradise flowers spread upon the floor. Pedro de Zanto seemed to know her as no one else ever had, and fear grew in her heart that he would soon guess that he meant more to her than a mere employer.

'If you are wondering, Jaine, if this apartment was to have been your cousin's, then let me assure you—'

'You don't have to, *senhor*.'

'Ah!' His black eyebrow took its sardonic arch. 'No communicating door, eh? And in the romantic fiction, which I am sure you read, there is always this door, making of the marriage a sort of bargaining counter for favours asked and

103

received. My child, you know very little about a man like me.'

'I – I admit that I know very little about men in general,' she said, trying hard not to sound too on the defensive.

'True,' he agreed. 'So let me enlighten you with regard to my own attitude with regard to marriage. If and when I marry there will be no doors of any sort between me and my wife, for such a relationship is for sharing, and that means of the off moments as well as the on. I shall not rap on any door for admittance to *my* woman, like a servitor asking for her indulgence. Ah, the colour comes into your cheeks, *senhorinha*. I make you blush with my Latin frankness.'

'Yes,' she admitted, for he pinned her upon his gaze like a helpless moth, and she could only pray silently that the servant would soon appear with the coffee and save her from these revelations that were amusing for him, and so disturbing for her. It was torture enough to know that one day another woman would have him, but it was fuel added to the flames to be given a resumé of how he intended to live personally with that most fortunate of females ... sharing everything with him, with no doors between them.

'I forget how innocent you are in a world where the only innocents are usually the newborn,' he drawled.

'I'm glad I amuse you,' she said, and she edged the folds of her robe over her bare ankles and feet, for their very bareness, with those unpainted toenails, seemed to add to her naïveté and lack of experience in dealing with a man ... and never in her wildest dreams had Jaine imagined a situation in which she would be alone in a bedroom with a man as worldly, as self-assured and physically attractive as the one who confronted her at the moment.

'Are you wondering if your innocence is in danger from me?' he inquired, and there was a gleam in his eyes that was not entirely one of mockery. Like a little tawny flame it flickered and also seemed to beckon, so that Jaine drew back imperceptibly against the cushions, as if somehow they might protect her instead of making it easier for him should he lean over her, should he bring those bold lips close to her.

As if reading her eyes and the fear they reflected he did lean forward and there was the faintest of smiles on his mouth. 'Innocence, curiously enough, provides its own protection,' he said. 'It disarms a man more effectively than all the experience in the world. All the same, *menina*, you are past the stage of being merely curious about men and you would like to know what makes them different from women – and I don't mean in the obvious sense.'

'I – I'm not curious about you—'

'I protest that you are.'

'And is that why you really came to my room, to test the extent of my curiosity?'

'Be careful you don't test the extent of my good will, Jaine.'

'Meaning that it's all right for you to – to psycho-analyse me, but I mustn't question any of your motives?'

'That is about it,' he said shamelessly. 'As a mere novice you are bound to attribute all the wrong motivations to anything I say and do, and you must learn to trust people. Do you know, Jaine, you are rather like a nervous little cat who has had a can tied to her tail, and I am doing my best to unloosen the knots which tie you to your inhibitions.'

'How – how kind of you,' she said, with a faint attempt at sarcasm.

'You will never know how kind,' he said enigmatically. 'It isn't usually in my nature to stop by the wayside to pick up a stray young cat. Perhaps I should take hold of you by the nape of the neck and give you a shake, eh?' And even as he spoke he curled a hand around Jaine's slim neck and pressed his fingers in under her ruffled hair, gripping her in such a way that she knew it would hurt furiously if she tried to resist him.

'How you would like to claw me and fight,' he mocked.

'Well, this is one of the differences between male and female.'

'Brute strength?' she flashed.

'What a bundle of nerve and fury you really are! No, little cat, the difference is that men and women enjoy this kind of thing. It is only when women antagonize each other that the fighting becomes painful and leaves traumatic bruises. You see, Jaine, at the very roots of things a man and a woman can never be true enemies, for they are each equipped to be lovers.' And as he spoke his fingers slid across her neck and left a little trail of fire along her collarbone. He knew well enough that he made his point without verification from Jaine, and he lazily turned his head as there came a soft knock upon the door, which opened to admit a young Indian in a crisp white tunic and trousers carrying a coffee tray. The Duque told him to bring the tray to the divan table, and because this time the Indian was a mere boy, Jaine felt the quick, inquisitive look which he gave her. He was not yet too dignified to be curious about the white girl whom the Duque had brought to Goldenhawk. For an instant she felt the jungle dark eyes on the pale skin of her throat in the pale green opening of her robe, and then he went hastily away at a sharp word from the Duque.

'You will be a source of curiosity,' he said. 'You do have an exceptionally white skin – look, my own arm seems swarthy against yours.'

Jaine glanced at the arm which he placed beside hers, but all she was really conscious of was the warmth of his skin and the brief pressure of his forearm muscles. Those arms placed around a woman would feel like iron and velvet at the same time, for their firm muscularity was overlaid by dark hair which brushed her skin and made her acutely aware of his maleness.

'Do pour the coffee before I die of thirst,' he urged, looking at her with that gleam of worldly amusement in his eyes. 'You will remember how I like it.'

'Black as tar, with one spoonful of sugar,' she rejoined, taking up the silver pot which was engraved with the hawk crest of the house. He had said that last time they had enjoyed coffee together that he liked it as black as his soul, but Jaine didn't quite believe that his soul was unrelieved of good deeds and kindly acts. It was written in his face, and an inheritance from the past, that he could be cruel at times, but she was learning that the sardonic mask concealed a sense of honour and humour. He did not attempt to whitewash his sins; he did not pretend to be a saint, and then reveal himself as a devil. As the coffee rose in the cups, she glanced at him, and it was again a shock to her system to find his eyes fixed upon her, curiously intent, and so tawny that their centres were like onyx ... black as night.

'This is a lovely coffee pot,' she said. 'There is nothing silver-plated at Goldenhawk, is there?'

'No,' he agreed. 'It is solid silver – old Indian and Portuguese silver, hand-hammered. The fruit dish is of silver and palm ivory, to match the cake-stand. You like things of quality, don't you, Jaine?'

'It's a sign of being under-privileged,' she replied, handing him his coffee, and using her lashes she avoided again a direct meeting with his eyes. She had not yet adjusted to the pace of his moods, and she had to keep reminding herself, for her own peace of heart, that he paid her to be here and it amused him to play the genial inquisitor. After all, his male life had been filled with attractive and enticing women, so why shouldn't he feel curious about their very opposite in the shape of herself – the odd little cat of Madge's description; the Pierrot, dark-capped and sad-eyed.

'You go without,' she added, 'to the point where you become – choosy.'

'A paradox, like yourself, Jaine.' He leaned back in his chair, stretched his long legs comfortably, and put his lips to the brim of his cup. 'Can you remember your parents at all?

107

Or were you too young when orphaned?'

'Too young, *senhor*.' She tasted her coffee, to which she had added cream, and found it like hot, sweet nectar.

'Good, eh?' He had seen the appreciative droop of her eyelids. 'There is nothing "instant" about the really worthwhile things of life. They are worth taking time and trouble over. Jaine, I am pleased you are not a superficial person, for Tristao is worth taking time and trouble over. He, too, has a certain sensitive quality that could be too easily bruised.'

'I am sure he has spirit as well, *senhor*.' Her lips would not be controlled of a smile. 'Tristao is your son.'

'He most certainly has the Zanto blood in his veins, but I have not been an altogether sensitive man, *senhorinha*. I have taken life by the horns, and you are not too innocent not to know that.'

'I'd be very foolish to imagine you in any role but that of a man who enjoys life,' she said. 'Are you afraid for the boy because of his – injury?'

'Concerned because of that, but also aware that he lacks my ruthless streak and yet may have to face a future less sure than my life has been. I was born here at Goldenhawk, and my adolescent years were bound to something that seemed as if it might last eternally. But in the last few years there have been great and sudden changes, and Tristao's path may veer away from the security I can give him for a while longer. Now and again I have to be away from Goldenhawk and that is why I wanted someone here – a woman who would become fond of him and care for his welfare. I thought in terms of a wife, but that was midsummer madness, a girl on a lawn with the sun in her hair, and that is the effect which being back in Portugal has upon a man. It evokes *saudade*, nostalgia for heaven knows what! When I met your cousin again, here in Brazil, the sun was harder and made a clearer image of her. And I think I must have shown her that the scales were off my eyes.'

'Something unnerved her,' Jaine agreed, and she kept her

gaze upon the dish of tamarinds and papayas, the exotic bananas with pinkish skins, arranged on a green palm leaf. 'And it isn't like my cousin to lose her nerve.'

He laughed softly, with irony in the sound. 'Thank the mother of faith you did not lose yours. If you have never eaten a pink banana, then please go ahead. I can see that you are fascinated.'

'Back in England we only get the West Indian variety.' She reached for one of the small, pretty fruits and carefully peeled it. She bit into it and was aware of the Duque's sardonic scrutiny. The banana was deliciously firm and sweet and flavoured, she knew, by the heady wine of being for this short while the *confianca* of a strong man who had let down his guard with her.

'You are afraid, eh, to reach out for the things you want?' With a lazy sureness he reached for a papaya and ate it. 'Yes, they are good. Much of what we have here is good to eat, good to look at, so enjoy your stay with us, Jaine.'

'I am sure I shall, *senhor*.' She spoke brightly and tried not to let it show that his words had about them an indefinite quality. He spoke as if she came on a visit and would have to leave in time. He had not allowed her to apply for a work permit. She was installed in the house, her things unpacked and hung in the closets, but nothing was to be regarded as permanent.

'The nights will seems strange at first,' he took up the coffee pot and refilled his cup. 'You will hear the baboons making for the river, and the scream of a doe when the black panther makes its kill. There are lone birds that utter strange cries and deep within the jungle the Indians hold their councils and when the wind is in this direction you will hear the drums. The jungle will seem a forbidding place at first, but when you have settled down and grown somewhat used to the heat, I will introduce you to some of the Mayan ruins, the remains of lost cities, and barbaric ritual. You will see strange plants and creepers, and may also have the luck to see the golden condor, the largest of all predatory birds that makes its home in this part of the world. Its wing span is incredible, and it has talons so powerful it can kill a panther. Our world is ruthless and beautiful at the same time. The Mayans say that it's a paradise guarded by monkeys to keep men from being too proud.'

'It's a world away from London, the River Thames, and the typewriter.' Jaine gave a little gasp of incredulity. 'Dare I pinch myself?'

'Allow me.' He leaned forward and quite deliberately he took her hand and nipped the tips of her fingers with his. 'There, you are awake and not dreaming, for I saw you flinch.'

'You have fingers of iron,' she said, but in reality she had felt his touch like a warm flame running up her arm into the bones of her body.

'And you are a very flimsy creature.' His eyes raked over her, then abruptly he climbed to his feet and strode across the room in the direction of the wall cupboards. He flung open the doors and examined the meagre contents, scattered there on the rails; the clothes from her suitcase.

'You are not a girl who feels she must keep up with the latest fashions, are you?' He shot the question at Jaine, who shook a slightly bewildered head.

'As I told you, I have a sister who took the veil in Portugal, but until that time she loved the fashion houses of Rio, and would even go as far as Lima to see a special designer of dress fabrics. Consequently her closets here at Goldenhawk are filled with an excellent range of her suits, dresses and various ensembles. I have never thought of disposing of them, and I have an idea there are garments you could make use of. It therefore seems a pity to let them hang useless — will you come and take look at them?'

He swung to look at her and he saw her hesitation. 'Have there already been too many hand-me-downs, Jaine?'

'It isn't that, *senhor*. Your sister might not like a stranger handling her things—'

'Magdalena would want someone to have them.' He spoke firmly and stood there with his hands thrust into his pockets, persuading her this time and not commanding her.

'But supposing—'

'She went away six years ago and is no longer a novitiate. Magdalena took her final vows eighteen months ago.'

'I see.' Janie bit her lip. 'It was a big step for her to take.'

'It followed upon the death of her fiancé. Unlike me, my sister is the faithful sort.' His smile was a brief twist of the lips. 'Latin women are often driven to degrees of sacrifice ... it seems to be in the blood. The order of the veil to which she belongs is a nursing one, so her life has purpose and is not spent in prayer and seclusion. I should not care to think of Magdalena shut up behind walls, all her beauty and love of life withering like a leaf upon a sunless tree. When Tristao and I went to Portugal those few months ago it was to see her for a short while. And now, Jaine, do you feel you could accept some of the contents of her stylish and scented closets? She was a young woman with impeccable taste – as you will see.'

'Very well, *senhor*.' Jaine rose from the divan, and she didn't feel as if she were being offered charity. The Duque was accustomed to seeing women in attractive clothes, and she felt strangely touched that he should want her to wear some of his sister's things. He was probably very fond of her and it would not have been easy for a man of his vital nature to accept his sister's decision to devote her life to strangers and never to have a family of her own.

'Her apartment is on the floor above this one, so I'll wait upon the balcony while you slip into a dress. For so long has this been a bachelor household that I forget some of the proprieties – I should not have exposed you to that boy's eyes in that robe, but with you, Jaine—' He walked to the doors of her balcony and opened them. He stepped outside, where the sun was flaming red in the sky and being drawn down towards the ocean. That red light bathed him in its fire, so that he seemed for an instant like a tall, powerful sun-god, smiling strangely as he went to the caged parapet of the *mirador* and stood there with his wide shoulders to Jaine.

With her he forgot to be the overriding male with an enticing woman – with her he relaxed to such a degree that her lightly clad body was no more than a boy's. It wasn't until that Indian boy had stared at her that Pedro had realized her femininity, her whiteness of skin, her flimsy girlishness.

Snatching a skirt and blouse from her wardrobe, Jaine stood within the shield of the big carved door and slipped off her robe, beneath which she wore only a slip and panties. She climbed into the skirt, buttoned up the blouse, and smoothed her hair with her hands.

She went to the *mirador* where he stood gazing at the red-shot sky. She didn't speak, but he sensed her presence. 'Come and look,' he said. 'Your first sunset at Goldenhawk, and it is a golden one indeed.'

Jaine stepped forward on to the balcony, towards the tall figure whose white shirt was a kaleidoscope of colour through the pierced openings of the *mirador*. The courtyard below was deepening with shadow and the many creepers had started to rustle in tune with the rasping of the cicadas, and the water of the pool had a jade and ruby glow. Jaine caught a whiff of the spicy scents, and she thought how graceful were the great palm fronds draping the husky trunks like green curtains, almost reaching to the ground. The *copihue* bells that had been so brightly red in the sun were now going as dark as velvet. When Jaine looked at the sky she caught her breath in wonder, for very gradually it was filling with colour like a painted ceiling, glowing with carmine, gold and palest mauve.

'It's more beautiful than anything I'd imagined,' she said softly.

'I must concede that it never fails to charm me.' His voice had also dropped into a lower note, and the effect was to make their being together in the enclosed balcony an intimate thing . . . to Jaine at least. Her fingers curled around the latticework of the *mirador* and never before had she felt so poignantly the wish that she might be the sort of girl who could charm a man. If she had such charm even the Duque wouldn't admire only the sunset and there on the skyline the tall Brazilian palms, erect, fronded, savagely beautiful.

'These boxed-in balconies are *mudejar*,' he said to her, 'from our Moorish origins. They were the people who implanted in us Latins a love of arabesqued tiling, intricate tracery of stone and ironwork, and those filigreed lamps you see being lit in the courtyard below us. See how they pattern the water of the pool and reveal like tapestries the flowered vines overhanging the walls? Yes, the Moors gave to us an eye for beauty, and the kind that seems more magical as dusk takes the day in its cloak and lets the night have its due. Soon the air will be heady with perfume from the flowers, who find the sun a little cruel and only start to breathe freely when darkness falls. Those big magnolias and roses will release their perfume like an incense, and the big moths will fly over our walls from the jungle, enticed by the glow of the lamps.'

He paused there and turned imperceptibly to face Jaine. 'The nights at Goldenhawk are always beautiful at this time of the year. You came at the right time, Jaine.'

'Yes, *senhor*,' she said politely. He would never know that she had come to Goldenhawk just as her lonely heart was ready to open itself, like those courtyard flowers. 'And I see what you mean – the night is kinder than the day, for it hides the blemishes.'

'On the contrary, Jaine, it reveals the hidden aspects of

places, and people. It is a paradox that the mask comes off at night and personalities undergo a subtle change. Breathe that air, *menina*, laced with the jungle. Dare you say that you are the same, reasonably self-controlled, shy young person I saw in the *sala* at the Casa de Rocha? I think not!'

'But I am,' she argued, and at once she knew it was a mistake to contradict him, for he swung fully to face her and his face was a golden mask, hard and mocking, with narrowed eyes, as he reached out and almost lifted her off her feet as he brought her tigerishly close to him.

'Now say it again, that you aren't more alive at this moment, in my hands, in my house, than you have been all the days of your life. Say it, Jaine!'

But she couldn't . . . her breath was half lost and a frightening sort of weakness swept over her as she felt her unawakened body crushed to his strong, supple frame that was so experienced when it came to women.

'Are you too frightened to speak?'

'Y-yes,' she managed to say. It had to be 'yes', for she could never tell him that it was love, not fear, that made her become so helpless when he touched her, the iron warmth of him thawing too quickly all the repressed longings and the unutterable loneliness of never being close to anyone. She was close to him now because she had angered him, but still it was a kind of heaven which she had to pretend was a kind of hell.

'So I frighten you?' His hands pressed against her waist, which was so slim that he could almost span it with his fingers. 'Yes, I could break you in half, could I not? A flimsy bit of bone and silk, with a certain rebellious fury banked down under the British ice. What is it, Jaine? Did you think of a Latin employer in terms of aloof courtesy even when annoyed? But this is Goldenhawk, on the edge of the jungle, and I was born within sound of its pagan rhythms. When I am angered I show my anger, just as when I am pleased I show my pleasure. It is you, Jaine, who represses what you feel.'

'It was the way I was brought up.' A little of her courage was coming back; the will and strength to keep her pride even if she had lost her heart. Her heart that was pounding beneath the thin stuff of her blouse and must be perceptible to him, who held her close to him so that he could mock her for a cold, repressed little virgin. 'It seems to me to be the correct behaviour for a companion, to be unobtrusive with her person and her opinions. It would hardly be correct if I suddenly shook off discretion and took to wearing a jungle flower in my hair. Or dancing in my bare feet. You did hire me, *senhor*, to take care of your son.'

'Yes, because I thought you young, and not yet ready for the shelf and scraps of uneventful data in the pages of a diary.'

'How – how do you know I keep a diary?' She tried to make the query sound off-hand, for she had a sudden nervous vision of him seeing that orchid pressed between the pages of her diary; so freshly pressed from his hand to hers.

'I saw it on the table beside the divan. I presume to guess that you had been entering the fact that today you came to Goldenhawk.'

'Yes,' she admitted. 'It isn't every day that someone like me comes to a house like this.'

'Someone like you, Jaine? What is so unusual about you?'

She flushed, for he seemed to be sardonic and faintly cruel as he looked at her in the last glimmers of pagan colour shed by the dying sun.

'I'm not exactly a picture of glamour,' she rejoined, on the defensive because his look had hurt her. 'Hardly as decorative as – well, no sort of substitute at all.'

'You were not brought here as a substitute for my bride,'

he drawled. 'Or did you suppose that you were?'

'Please – don't be cruel.' She flinched with pain as she tried to wrench herself away from him and his grip fastened, fingers of steel pressing into her body. 'Y-you twist my words, my meaning, and all because I disagreed with you on a very minor issue. You act the tyrant!'

'Act, Jaine?' He stared down into her eyes, like one of those gold-eyed, sleek black panthers mesmerizing its intended prey. 'I am being myself, Pedro de Zanto. It is he who has hold of you, who speaks to you as if you are a thing of flesh instead of a mere doormat, to be walked on, shaken, used, discarded when worn out. I speak, argue, and rant at you because I take you for an intelligent female who wants more from any man than to be treated and looked at as if part of the furnishings. And I am disappointed that you take it as tyranny. That you want an employer in place of a – friend.'

His words shook her deeply ... she was so used to being bullied that she had thought he was following the pattern already so well set by Madge, and even by Laraine. She hadn't dreamed that he wanted friendship and not servility.

She was looking at him, her heart shaken, when he abruptly withdrew his hands from her waist and left a coldness where there had been a branding warmth.

'So, Jaine, in some measure you will be my *confianca* as well. A house gets lonely when the sun goes down and darkness slips in through the windows, and you will eat at my table, take coffee and *conac* each evening with me, and talk to me. I intend to know you – in the short while permitted to us.'

Her heart seemed to turn and to sink. 'The – the post is not permanent, *senhor*?'

'As permanent as anything can be these days. Come, let us go and find you some dresses for evening wear – and, Jaine, never be afraid to be outspoken and fearless with me. I shan't take a whip to you.'

Jaine managed to smile . . . he wasn't to know that it was like being whipped to learn that her stay at Goldenhawk was to be only an interlude in her life.

CHAPTER EIGHT

THEY mounted the stairs to the corridor where the Duque's sister had had her apartment; the wall lights had now been turned on, and Jaine was told casually that the estate had its own electricity system, though in bad weather the generator sometimes failed and oil-lamps were then used for illumination.

The corridor was lined with heavily carved cedarwood doors, and Jaine felt a slight sensation of coldness, as though she sensed a ghostly presence; that of the youthful Magdalena, perhaps, who had brought the place alive with her gaiety and beauty. Now she was far away, and to all this she had become a stranger. This grace and grandeur; liveried Mayan servants with dark handsome eyes, and a brother who still showed signs of missing his sister. Apart from Tristao he seemed to have no other close relative.

A house was lonely, he had said, when the sun went down. Jaine sensed that loneliness as he paused in front of one of the carved doors and seemed to brace his shoulders before turning the handle and opening the door.

As the central light sprang into life, Jaine was aware at once that the interior of the room was beautiful and unique. Here the furniture was not heavy and colonial, but styled in pale golden woods inlaid with tulipwood. Everything had grace, set against the lavishly draped curtains of a silvery blue. The feet sank into a carpet that matched the curtains, and the long triple bedroom mirrors reflected the silver and crystal containers upon the toilet-table. Though the room had not been used for so long it was in a spotless condition; as cared for as if the Duque still hoped that one day Magdalena would return to Goldenhawk.

He walked past a little table upon which stood a white

pearwood dove, and he slid open the doors of the long wardrobe. At once a selection of beautiful clothes sprang into view, and Jaine's nostrils tensed to the perfume and the cedarwood combined, and she guessed that it was the lining of cedarwood which had kept the wardrobe airtight and the contents free from damage by moths or termites.

The Duque stared a moment at the long rack of lovely things, as if his memory still held images of Magdalena clad in this dress or that. Then with a frown he turned away and beckoned Jaine into the adjoining sitting-room, where once again the furnishings were graceful and original, designed to give comfort to the body and pleasure to the eye. As Jaine gazed round at the softly gleaming furniture and the subtle colours of the fabrics it struck her that Magdalena had been a person both sensuous and fond of lovely things – yet she had chosen to enter a nunnery, where personal comfort was kept to the minimum, and where the body, no matter how shapely, was covered by the habit and the veil. And where the emotions were channelled into self-sacrifice rather than self-indulgence.

There was absolutely no doubt that the Duque's sister had enjoyed stylish clothes and fine possessions. There on a divan table was a Greek goddess of ivory riding nude on a sea-monster. There was a striking red carpet with a motif of pure white leaves. Cardinal-red cushions glowed against the dove-grey velvet of the divan, and a white Hepplewhite desk graced an alcove of the room with its tiers of drawers and wrought-iron decoration.

'That was Magdalena.' The Duque directed Jaine's attention to the pale gold panelling of a nearby wall, and a little arrow of shock seemed to pierce Jaine as she met the painted eyes of the girl in the ivory picture frame. Jaine stared at the tilt of the eyes, beautiful and catlike, gold and vivid set within the silky black lashes. The face itself was vivid rather than truly beautiful, but her slim body was lovely, set off by the passion-red dress which she wore, so simple in design and yet so striking, with a single huge white orchid nestling against the graceful folds of the skirt.

The Cristata orchid, Jaine thought instantly, from the heart of the jungle. Yes, this girl would love orchids and they would become her, for there was something exotic about her smooth blue-black hair, her pale gold skin, and her deep gold eyes. Her mouth . . . that alone was like a scarlet flower, wearing the faintest of sensuous smiles.

'She was lovely,' Jaine breathed, 'and she reminds me of Tristao – of your son, *senhor*.'

'Of course,' he said suavely. 'And why not, when she is my sister?'

'I can see,' Jaine dared to say, 'why you find it hard, even after all this time, to accept all that she gave up to become a nun. The high white walls, the quiet corridors, the bells and prayers must all be very different from what she had – loved, here at Goldenhawk.'

'The order to which she belongs is known as the Virgen de la Soledad.' There was a strange note of irony in the Duque's deep voice. 'I knew Magdalena so well that even yet I cannot imagine that she is fully happy, fulfilled and content. I am, as I told you, neither saint nor satan. I cannot help but believe that the best of happiness comes to any woman through a bond of love with a man, but my sister believed that she would never again find that love after she lost it – she was ill, then when she recovered she ran away from Brazil and the next thing I heard was that she was at the House of the Virgin of the Solitude, in Portugal. I tried to persuade her to return home with me when I flew there to see her. She refused – became quite hysterical. The Mother Superior of the Order advised me to wait a while, to see which way Magdalena would go, the way of the veil, or the way of the world.'

He shrugged his wide shoulders and spread his lean hands in a very Latin gesture. 'I may shock you when I say that I believe that had Magdalena allowed me to bring her away from the Priory that night, she would not have returned. Stay in Portugal, I said to her. There are friends there for you. You have no need to come to Brazil ever again – but she wept and cried so much she alarmed me. A man doesn't like or understand tears, *senhorinha*, not when he has done all that he can for someone, and still she weeps as if her heart had broken and her world was in ruins. She had always been so – so gay of spirit that I never thought she would take it so much to heart when her fiancé came to grief in Peru. It never seemed to me that she was a girl who could become so intensely involved with a man – there seemed so many other things that she enjoyed – life, clothes, riding, the restaurants of Rio and the theatres. I sometimes wonder if she would have been so bereft had there not—'

There, abruptly, he broke off in mid-sentence, and just as abruptly left the sitting-room and returned to the bedroom, where the wardrobe still stood open.

With a kind of restrained savagery the Duque collected an armful of the elegant and stylish garments. 'Come,' he said. 'These should do, and as you are about the same age and weight as Magdalena when they were made for her, they will not need much adjustment to your own figure. It is also fortunate that you have the brunette hair – a softer shade than hers, but the colours she preferred will suit you. The jewel colours – ruby, garnet, beryl, and especially the gem-green. You have never dressed up your white skin and your emerald eyes, but now you will, Jaine. Now I give the order and you will obey it – you called me a tyrant, did you not?'

Jaine followed his long strides from the room, switching off the light behind her, closing the door, leaving that portrait all alone in the dark; that glowing, sensuous, cat-eyed girl who would never more smile for a man and seduce him with her golden gaze.

The Duque arrived at Jaine's door ahead of her and striding in he dropped the armful of dresses on to the bed, where they lay in a dazzling heap against the pale lace of the bed-spread.

'Now they are yours,' he said crisply. 'They have no other owner, for Magdalena is now Sister Maria and she has no further use for finery, or the pains and pleasures of our world. Which is best, I wonder?' His eyes glinted and held Jaine's gaze inexorably. 'Would you go into a nunnery if the world turned against you, Jaine?'

'I – I don't know, *senhor*.' She stood there with such gravity and politeness that her inner tumult was visible only in the clenching of her hands behind her, so hard that her fingers hurt. 'I have never been the kind of person to become involved in a tragic romance. Your sister was incredibly attractive, but I don't attract men, *senhor*.'

The tawny eyes swept over her, not missing a detail of her person. He turned to the bed and plucked from the heap of garments a long dress of exquisite green velvet. 'Wear this,' he said, 'and you might have cause to change your opinion of yourself. As a jewel is flattered by the right setting, so is a woman flattered by the right gown. Clever dressmakers get rich, *senhorinha*, because they know that beauty is intrinsic rather than obvious and they know how to reveal it . . . just as Nature will reveal her flowers at the correct time of the year.'

With these words he was at the door, and with an incli-nation of his dark head he was gone. Jaine didn't move from her position for several minutes . . . she still felt dazed, as if she had passed through a whirlwind of impressions and emotions.

Well, it wouldn't do just to stand here and gape at the mound of dresses on the bed; she had better hang them in her wardrobe before they became crumpled. As she handled each one she grew less and less certain that she would ever find the nerve to wear such garments. It wasn't a matter of pride because they had belonged to another girl; she could tell, in fact, that some of them had not yet been worn. It was just that she was so used to thinking of herself as a colour-less person that she would surely look a sparrow trying to pass herself off as a canary if she dared to wear a dress made for someone who had been vivid to look at and sure of herself.

Jaine stroked the lovely skirt of a flounced dress embroidered in silver and green at the hem, in a pattern of flowers and shells in the most intricate needlework. The bodice was also embroidered and the silk material rustled in her hands. She swiftly put the dress away, for it was so glamorous, designed to be worn to the theatre and a meal for two at a candlelit supper-club.

But the next dress which Jaine picked up she held against her . . . it was the deep green one of the Duque's selection, in a supple velvet, long and flowing and almost gothic with its monk-sleeves, and cowled neckline. Jaine could see how the colour blended with her eyes, but she would surely never have the nerve to wear it. On Magdalena it would have been the essence of seduction, but Jaine felt sure that on her the gothic styling would create an effect of green-shaded cloisters and vesper bells. A smile moved her lips, which the mirror reflected. A pensive and questioning smile, too swift for lingering, the edge of a moth-wing, flown off before it could be captured.

She shook her head at herself, and yet she could feel the quick, nervous beating of her heart, and the excitement running in her veins. Wear them, he had ordered. They are yours!

Mine, she thought, in which to masquerade as a lady of finery for a couple of hours each evening. How Madge would smile, and how scornfully Laraine would laugh. Oh yes, there had been hand-me-downs from Laraine, but nothing as fabulous as this collection of couture gowns, made for the sister of a *duque*, who had discarded them in favour of the dark habit and the white coif.

Jaine firmly closed the wardrobe door and shut away in

the darkness the glimmering gowns. For now she would forget about them. Tristao would be awake by now and ready for his evening meal.

When she entered his bedroom he was seated in the centre of his bed, wide awake and playing with a model of a Silver Hurricane, diving in and out of his bedcovers with a lot of vocal noise. He grinned as he caught sight of her and held up the plane for her inspection. 'Do you like it, *senhorinha*? It was bought for me by Papa when we were in Portugal, at the English toyshop on the big *avenida* in Lisbon. Is it not beautiful? So smooth and shiny, and look at the guns in the firing turrets!'

'It truly is a masterpiece,' she smiled, as she sat down on the edge of his bed and looked at him. His dark hair was ruffled into the very smallest curls, and his golden eyes were bright after his long and restful nap. Yes, how very much he resembled the Duque's sister. Those eyes, that pointed chin, the little dents under the cheekbones. It was no wonder his father had kept him, clung to him, bound him legally no matter what people said, or what the mother's position had been. He had wanted the boy at any cost, and Jaine could only suppose that the mother had been so well provided for that she had not disputed the Duque's claim on Tristao.

Had she not seen the wording of the Zanto armorial crest and understood the meaning? *'Take with force, and keep with honour!'*

'How about getting dressed and having something to eat?' she asked the boy. 'You must be feeling hungry, Tristao. Do you fancy anything special that I can order for you?'

He considered the question, stroking a finger up and down the smooth wing of his aeroplane, his eyes fixed intently upon Jaine's face. 'Will you eat with me?' he asked. 'I usually have to eat in the nursery all alone, for Papa dines very late, and then he is often busy in the study. Do you like my papa, *senhorinha*?'

The question startled her, but she quickly readjusted to it. The boy was only asking from a childish angle and she would have to get used to being questioned by this curious, rather lonely, and intelligent child.

'He is a very courteous gentleman, Tristao. I very much respect him,' she replied. 'And I can tell that he loves you dearly.'

'Have you no papa who loves you?' Tristao inquired, leaning forward as if to see himself reflected in her green eyes.

'My father died a long time ago,' she said, touching a finger to a curl on the smooth olive brow. 'I don't remember him, but I feel sure he was very nice.'

'And your mama – she is dead like mine?'

This time the question shook Jaine's heart, for she knew from what the Duque had told her that Tristao's mother was very much alive. She could only suppose that Pedro had thought it better to let his son assume that his mother was gone irrevocably out of his life, but all the same ... all the same it did seem rather ruthless to separate the son so decisively from the mother. No longer in love with her, was the Duque afraid that she might steal some of the boy's affection? Was he really so arrogant that he couldn't endure the thought of sharing what he loved with another human being? Or was it that having lost the companionship of Magdalena he was anxious that nothing should come between him and the boy? Jaine suppressed a little sigh and felt that she would never truly understand this subtle and unfathomable man whom her untutored heart had chosen to love.

'Now what are you going to have for your tea?' She picked up Tristao's slippers and fitted them to his feet, noticing with concern the slight deformation of his lame leg.

'I think I should like *blinis*,' he said, 'with hot butter and jam.'

'They sound nice,' she said. 'I suppose it will be all right if I ring for them? I am still a little uncertain of etiquette in your household, Tristao, and I don't wish to annoy the staff.'

'Papa will have told them that you are my Miss Dare,' he said, importantly. 'I will ring the bell and Justus will come in answer and I will tell him about the *blinis*, until you get used to things, *senhorinha*.'

'*Muito obrigado, senhorito*,' she said, keeping her face straight. 'You are most kind, especially in view of the fact that my Portuguese is almost nil and I am going to have difficulty in communicating with the staff for a while. Do any of them speak English, apart from your father's very dignified *major-domo*?'

'No, they all speak in dialect apart from Primitivo, but they are very good at understanding signs,' Tristao told her eagerly. 'That is because they come from the jungle, where most of the talking is made in signs so they make no noise when they are hunting. Papa says that the Mayas have eyes and ears as sharp as the puma. He knows, for he has often hunted with them. When I grow up a little more he will take me along, but we will not be able to take you with us, *senhorinha*, for the Mayas don't like girls to go hunting.'

'I shan't mind that,' Jaine couldn't help glancing at the big tawny jaguar skin beside the boy's bed, with head and teeth fiercely intact. 'It seems cruel to me, though I suppose some of these animals are killers.'

'Yes, rogue killers.' Tristao kneeled down and took the jaguar head into his arms. 'Papa shot this big fellow, who had dragged children into the jungle. Look, you can see where the bullet went right into the brain, so the cat did not suffer, and the pelt was not damaged. Papa is a man of great experience.'

'I am sure he is,' Jaine said dryly. 'Now ring for your tea, and see that you wash your hands and face properly while I make myself acquainted with your lesson and your leisure books. Have you had any sort of companion or tutor before me, Tristao?'

He turned from the press-bell and shook his head. 'Papa sets lessons for me and listens when I read. I go to his study for two hours every day, except when he has to be away—' Tristao frowned and gnawed his underlip. 'Sometimes he goes in the night and I don't know about it. He never used to do this, *senhorinha*. Is it because of all this extra business that he has asked you to be my *confianca*?'

'Of course,' she smiled. 'Your father doesn't like leaving you, but I expect it is unavoidable when a man has so many irons in the fire.'

'What are irons in the fire?' Tristao blinked his eyes in astonishment at Jaine. 'Papa deals in coffee and minerals and land, not in irons, *senhorinha*.'

'It's a saying we have in England, Tristao. It means that your father has many financial interests and he likes to keep them hot to handle.' Very hot, she thought, if he flew off in the nights in order to handle his various deals. Or did he have some other reason for his nocturnal departures? Was he involved in a love affair that could not be explained to the boy, yet which would explain the Duque's sudden need for a day and night companion for Tristao; someone who would be available when he was absent.

Jaine felt a strange little ache in the region of her heart. It had to be expected that a man such as the Duque did not live as if he were a monk, and she would have to learn to accept both sides of his personality. There were people he needed as friends, and she was one of those. There were women he desired, and she was not among them. To them he gave his charisma and his flattery, but to her he gave the care of his son, and that in itself was something to cherish.

'Hands and face,' she said briskly to Tristao, in order to hide the fact that she felt like hugging the small, dark-haired figure to that ache in her heart. He looked very young and thin as he stood there in his silk pyjamas, and this prompted her to say that he had better have the *blinis* for dessert and perhaps for starters some of that delicious pastry she had tasted the other day, stuffed with meat, onion and tomatoes, with a few small potatoes baked in cheese. 'You must be feeling as hungry as I am, *amigo*,' she added, with a coaxing smile.

'You are going to eat with me?' he asked. 'And that is what you fancy, *senhorinha*?'

'I do indeed.' As she spoke someone knocked on the nursery door. It was the boy Justus, who had come in answer to the bell. She nodded at Tristao, and he rattled off their order for tea in the dialect that Jaine felt sure she was never going to learn. '*Sim, senhorito.*' The Mayan boy slid his intensely dark eyes to Jaine's face, giving her a long stare that she met gravely. Earlier on she knew that his youthful curiosity had been rebuked by the Duque, but she understood that the Mayas would be curious about her, and because she wanted their friendship she had to suppress the slight nervousness which even Justus aroused in her. She, with her Celtic skin and eyes, was as strange to them as they were to her, but if she showed nervousness instead of dignity she felt sure these proud Indians would despise her.

She stood there, her chin tilted and her spine very straight, the strangeness of all this tightly locked inside her. Then Justus said something to Tristao, gave a courteous little bow and left the nursery.

Jaine glanced inquiringly at Tristao, who gave her his puckishly solemn grin. 'Justus says that you have eyes like the dragon-stones that come out of the ground. He means emeralds, *senhorinha*.'

'Well,' she gave a slight laugh, 'I don't quite know how to take that. I hope I don't seem a dragon ... you are truly happy to have me here, *amigo pouco*?'

Tristao's answer was to limp over to Jaine, to take her

hand and to press it to his cheek. It was a gesture that needed no words, and it stole away Jaine's few remaining doubts about coming here to Goldenhawk. The boy needed her, and she was glad she had dared to come, even if it meant that recovery from what she felt for his father was now unlikely. She would have to endure the pain and ecstasy of that as best she could . . . at least she would not have spent her entire life in the dull backwaters of existence, where one performed one's daily duties just for bread and board. For now, and for the foreseeable future, this flame had lit up her life, and it was exciting, tempestuous, almost a game, to love and never by a look or a word betray the presence of it. A betrayal could only cause embarrassment for her, and for the Duque.

'What of you, *senhorinha*?' Tristao gripped her hand. 'Are you happy that you are here? You will stay and not go away – not too soon?'

'Not too soon,' she promised, for the child sensed, as she knew, that her stay was not to be one without an end in sight. Perhaps his father had dropped a hint to that effect. 'Tomorrow you must show me lots more of Goldenhawk, but right now we'll get you ready for your tea, and afterwards choose a book to start reading together. I bet you enjoy the same sort of books as I do, all about exploration and brave deeds.'

He nodded and was still gripping her hand as they entered the bathroom together. There she discovered that he had a big tub sunk into the floor, rather too big for so small a boy, and a shelf of boats for floating about in the water when he took his bath. 'I hope,' she said, as she filled the porcelain bowl with warm water, 'that you have someone with you when you have your bath?'

'I am not a baby,' he protested. 'I learned to swim a long time ago, for Papa was told it was good for my leg. Papa is usually here to see that I dry myself properly, and when he is busy, Justus looks after me.'

'I see.' Jaine soaped a flannel and proceeded to wash his face and hands, having heard that small boys took a cat's lick and a promise when it came to the face, though they didn't mind going into a tub where they could splash about. She handed him a face towel, and after he emerged from it she asked a question which had been faintly bothering her:

'Tristao, have you never had a woman to look after you before I came to Goldenhawk?'

'Yes, when I was very young. It was because of her that I—' The boy bit his lip and glanced down at his leg. 'The gardening boy at the house of Tia Felicia told me about her – he said that she took me out in a car and drove it into a wall. I do sort of remember the glass and being pinned down and how much it hurt. My *tia* who is a nun came from Portugal to sit beside me at the hospital, and Papa had tears in his eyes. My leg never got really better, but I don't get pain from it the way I did. That is one good thing.'

'Yes, darling, one good thing.' Jaine gently combed his black and rather curly hair. 'Do you know what happened to your nurse?'

'Sancho, the gardening boy for Tia Felicia, told me that she was killed dead. He said that Tia Felicia said it was a good thing, otherwise Pedro would have finished her. Pedro is my papa.' Tristao suddenly broke into a devilish little grin. 'My papa has a very enormous temper, and Justus says that when the Excellency's eyes are like the jungle cat's and about to spit fire, then it is best to hide in the potato cupboard.'

Jaine couldn't suppress a grin of her own at the description, yet behind her amusement there lay a sense of the tragedy which had almost occurred for Pedro de Zanto. If the boy had been killed and the woman had lived, Jaine felt sure he would have let loose his terrible temper on her. It was no wonder that for so long he had distrusted the care that a woman might take of his son ... why he had been so impressed when she had run in front of his car in order to snatch a child to safety.

She and Tristao returned to his bedroom, where he put on his dressing-gown and they sat at the nursery table and ate the very tasty meal which Justus brought on a tray. Tristao wanted to hear all about London, and was Big Ben a giant, and did the Queen still sail in her barge up and down the River Thames.

Jaine discovered the delight of a child's company; to such a degree that it was well past Tristao's bedtime when she finally got him tucked down. In his bookcase she found a copy of *Gulliver's Travels*, printed in English, with on the fly-leaf a dedication which read: 'To my boy Pedro, with best love from Mama.' A favourite book handed down from father to son, and one which Jaine handled with a very secret pleasure. As a boy Pedro had read this book, or had listened as dreamily as Tristao to the soft voice of a woman, before falling off to sleep.

She closed the book and studied the sleeping face against the white pillow, in the corner of which was the embroidered crest of the Zanto family. A golden hawk with its talons hooked around a sword and a lily.

The boy's lashes were like dark silk against the olive smoothness of his thin young cheek. His lips had a childish droop to them ... lips that would harden, grow firmer as the years went by, until one day he was a man, who would, perhaps, remember only vaguely the English girl who came to Goldenhawk to keep him company for a while.

Her breath caught on a little sighing smile and she rose from the bedside and returned the book to its niche in the bookcase. Fairly new books nudged spines with old books and showed promise of lots of entertaining reading for Tristao and herself. *A Golden Treasury of Fables, Tales of King Richard and the Crusades, Explorations of Peru* – she took out this volume and as she opened it a folded piece of paper fell from between the pages. Jaine picked it up and saw at once that it was part of a letter. She replaced it in the book, for curious as she was about this family, she drew the line at putting her eye to a keyhole.

Peru, that land of Inca ruins and strange legends, was where Magdalena had lost her fiancé to fatal accident in one of the old temples, and Jaine felt again that a certain shadow of sadness lay over this Brazilian family . . . as if long ago a curse might have been cast, haunting the tawny stones of Goldenhawk, and walking silent at the heels of the Duque de Zanto and those with his blood in their veins.

A shiver ran through Jaine and she slid the Peruvian book back into place and returned to the side of Tristao's bed. He slept peacefully, with the soft nursery light falling across his slight figure in the bed, which in the tradition of a ducal house had carving upon it and a light silk canopy to keep out the draughts at night. Jaine bent down and very carefully she brushed her lips across his hair. He stirred just a little and murmured a name . . . Papa.

As Jaine made her way to her own apartment, she wondered why the Duque had not been up to wish the boy good night. She had thought earlier that she had caught the sound of hoofbeats down in the courtyard, so it could be that he had a visitor, or had gone out himself. Feeling a trifle restless, Jaine decided to take a quiet stroll back and forth along the gallery where portraits hung and where she would not be noticed. She was not yet confident enough of her position here to venture down into the patio, and there was every chance that if the Duque entertained a visitor they would be smoking their cigars out there, among the flowering creepers and under the stars.

Jaine walked the gallery, gazed upon by the ancestral eyes of the Duque's forebears. Proud and aloof as the sitters of portraits always are, as if conscious that they must impart the importance of the family by looking gloomy rather than gay. Then again Jaine had to remember that she was looking at women chosen to be the brides of the Zanto men. Selected like well-trained fillies for the honour, blinkered against the little adventures their spouses indulged in.

The marriage of selectivity was still indulged in by Latin people, and Jaine wondered what her cousin Laraine was thinking at this precise moment. She knew by now that Jaine was here at Goldenhawk, and she would probably toss her golden head and say that he had wanted to marry *her*, but Jaine was no more than a servant in his house.

She paused in the shadows at the far end of the gallery, where a window was lavishly curtained and deeply embrasured. Jaine sat down on the wide sill and thought to herself that the lonely night all around the house was a well for all sounds. A rustling of leaves, the pad of a manservant's footsteps, the cough of a puma, the shirring of a night bird's wings. The sounds were strange as yet, and she had to learn them, as she might learn music. They touched her nerves and her senses as nothing had touched her in the household of her aunt . . . it was there that she had been the servant, and made to feel inferior because she wasn't pretty, or clever in a brittle way, and able to be decorative at a cocktail party.

Jaine's lips formed a little moue of distaste as she recalled those parties, at which she served like a maid, taking round the drinks, picking up scraps of gossip, and aware all the time that her heart longed for something more than this attendance upon sychophants and drifters from one idle pleasure to another. She had never made any attempt to be part of those pleasures, and in many ways it had suited Madge to treat her as a servant rather than a niece.

Now she could be glad of that, for her severance from the old life hurt no one. There had been no ties of affection . . . it was only since coming to Goldenhawk that she had begun to come truly alive, like a plant feeling the sun on its leaves for the first time.

So absorbed in her thoughts was she that she gave a distinct start as a long shadow fell across her seated figure. She quickly turned her head, expecting to see one of the servants. Instead she saw the master of the house, clad in a wine-velvet smoking jacket over dark trousers, a drift of smoke from the cigar in his fingers. Jaine gazed speechless at the crisp black hair, strong slanting cheekbones, and the eyes made so vivid by the darkness of his lashes and brows.

'So there you are,' he said. 'I hope you have eaten, Jaine?'

'Yes, thank you, *senhor*. I had supper with Tristao.'

'Good. I had an unexpected visitor, otherwise you would have dined downstairs in the *salon* with me. The talk was all of – business, and I thought you might find it tedious. Tristao ate a good meal?'

'Yes, I'm really glad to say that he did.' She smiled, though the shock of this man's compelling distinction was still knocking at her heart and causing little tremors to her nerves which she hoped were not visible to him. 'For his dessert he ate four whole *blinis* with butter and jam.'

'Ah yes, he has a fondness for those little pancakes, to which he was introduced by one of his doctors, a rather clever Russian. I brought back the recipe for our chef here, for sometimes the child's appetite can be capricious.' The cigar was raised to the bold lips with a fine chiselling to their outline, smoke was drawn in and exhaled by the proud nostrils. 'I always had the hope that his leg might be completely mended, for his sake, *senhorinha*, and not from any selfish feeling of my own. But unfortunately there is a slight paralysis of the ankle tendon, and complete recovery is impossible. I might add that I am grateful he was spared his young life, but I have ceased to take him to the various doctors. It builds up hopes which I know can only be shattered again. He is a sweet-natured child, eh? Uncomplaining and lovable.'

'Very much so,' Jaine agreed warmly. 'He and I are

friends already. In fact he told me—' She broke off and looked hesitant. 'I wasn't prying, but it did come out how he came to be hurt.'

'I quite agree that you should know. He was three and I had placed him in the care of a nurse because of my business commitments. We were living in my house at Rio at the time, and I made no objection to the woman having a car and taking Tristao with her on drives to the shops and the beach. I did not wish to wrap him in cottonwool and to make a baby of him, for in this world of ours a boy has to grow up to be self-assured and aware of life. I was at my office when the news came to me – there had been an accident, the car had crashed into a wall near the sea-front where the roads go downhill. The nurse was dead of a broken neck, and it was thought at first that the boy would die. At the hospital I was able to supply blood for a transfusion, being fortunately of the same blood group, and as the hours went by he became gradually stronger and was able to undergo surgery on his poor mangled leg. *Nom de deus*, what agony it is to sit and wait and wonder if what you love – and it was then I realized how much I did love that child – is to live or die, and he had lived but three short years!'

This time the Duque's pull upon the cigar was extremely deep and the smoke that he exhaled made a blue cloud about his head. 'Ever since those days I have had Tristao with me as often as possible. It is only recently that I – well, it is sufficient to say that I am glad to have you here, Jaine. I am gratified that you have made such friends with the boy. I thought there was something about you that might appeal to a child – a certain kindness of heart, allied to those great green eyes of yours. I wish that I could have found you sooner, Jaine.'

Her heart gave a little lurch at the words, even as she realized what he meant. Had Tristao been in her care when he was three years of age, the accident in the car and the injury to his leg might not have occurred.

'Why are you sitting here?' The Duque glanced around him at the wall-lamp shadows thrown on to the panelling, and at the portraits that gazed upon her with such indifferent eyes. 'Don't you care for your apartment?'

'Oh yes, it's very nice, *senhor*, but I was looking at the portraits and I just happened to see this window-seat.' She smiled tentatively. 'There is something about a window-seat, especially at night. It's a sort of shield between the darkness, and the things unseen that linger in a very historic house.'

'Yes, the house has been witness to quite a lot of – history.' His smile was faintly ironic. 'But there are draughts, Jaine. The nights grow cool because a tropic sun is always a hot one. Come with me to the *sala* and take a glass of wine before you retire.'

He held out a hand to assist her from the window-seat, and she fought not to betray her acute sensitivity to his touch as the lean fingers closed around hers and she felt the pressure of his ring. As he drew her to her feet, clad in a very simple grey-green dress of her own, with inexpensive pale-green beads about her throat, Jaine was so aware of the moment that she felt certain she would remember it all her life.

'Your hand is cold,' he said. 'You need that glass of wine.'

'I – I really would prefer to go to bed, *senhor*.' It took nearly all her resolve to refuse him. 'I have had a long day, and I never do have really warm hands.'

'Cool hands and a warm heart, is that it, Jaine?' He forced her to meet his eyes, and because there were tiny shadows of fatigue beneath her eyes, he submitted to her wish and escorted her to the door of her bedroom.

'Then I will say *boa moite, senhorinha*, and insist that you take that glass of wine another time.'

'Thank you, *senhor*. Good night.'

He opened her door and she entered her room. He gave

her a brief bow and swung on his heel, and all she took of him as she closed the door was the scent of his cigar. It had entered with her and it lingered in a subtly tormenting way.

CHAPTER NINE

SEVENTEEN days had passed and it still seemed amazing to Jaine that she was living in a house on the verge of the jungle, for so far she had not really seen it ... only from a distance, when she and Tristao spent time on one of the upper terraces of Goldenhawk.

He was in her care from nine in the morning until noon, when they had lunch. For an hour or so after lunch Tristao would take a nap in his room, then he would spend some time with the Duque, who was teaching him the history of the Portuguese and the rudiments of mathematics, at the end of which time he was in Jaine's care again.

It was a pleasant routine and one she liked, but now she had grown accustomed to the house and its various patios and gardens, Jaine was beginning to get curious about the countryside beyond the rambling walls of Goldenhawk. She had the feeling that the Duque preferred her to keep Tristao and herself within the security of those walls – no doubt he was still on thorns in case she proved as reckless as that other nurse – and Jaine guessed that for a while longer she had better abide by his unspoken wish.

But it all looked so wildly beautiful and beckoning, and Jaine decided that one evening she would find the nerve to ask the Duque if she could explore a little beyond his walls. She could always take her ramble during Tristao's siesta, and she would certainly promise not to venture too far among those wonderful towering trees, laced all over with vines and hung with all those exotic wild flowers. From the terrace it looked like a green Eden, and perhaps in her heart she hoped he would remember his promise to show her the jungle himself.

Because there was a bathing-pool in the grounds themselves, she and the boy used it in preference to the beach and the sea. The beach could only be reached from a twisting pathway of rather rough steps and this meant that one of the Mayas would have to carry Tristao. Jaine knew that Tristao hated any emphasis on his lameness, and it also seemed to her that the sea looked cold . . . though this fact did not seem to deter the Duque, and more than once she had caught sight of him returning from a morning plunge, clad informally, with a towel slung over his shoulders, and his hair as gleaming black as a raven's wing.

When she dined at his table in the evenings, he was always very formal, clad in a black dinner-jacket, or wearing sometimes a crisp white one that made him seem unnervingly big and dark.

It had taken considerable nerve for Jaine to start wearing the dresses which he had forced upon her, but after taking the plunge, and selecting the most simplest gowns, Jaine felt a deep, shy pleasure in being so well dressed for those evenings in the company of the Duque. His chef was an excellent one and there was always a variety of dishes, some Portuguese, some deliciously French, and some that were English . . . to make her feel at home, or because the Duque had developed a liking for roast beef and vegetables during his college years in England.

She had known before coming here of the worldly side of his nature, but she now learned how thoroughly cultured he was. He knew a tremendous amount regarding art, music and literature. And he seemed quite happy to expand Jaine's horizon with regard to this upper level of knowledge, which had never come her way during her years with Madge, who had been interested only in the theatre of light entertainment.

The Duque's extensive library was thrown open to Jaine, and when she sincerely thanked him, he dryly replied that the more she learned of the classics, the more Tristao learned.

Sometimes after dinner, which was always a leisurely meal in the Latin tradition, for he was obviously a connoisseur of good food and excellent wine, they would go to his study for coffee instead of entering the *sala* with its beautiful furniture, wide spaces, and elegant carpets. The panelled walls of the study were thick with paintings, engravings, landscapes and impressions carried out in the old and the new forms. There wasn't one that didn't have merit of value, and the Duque seemed to enjoy letting Jaine in on the secret of what made a painting a work of art.

In very short order she had grown to value those evenings in his study beyond gold or gems. She not only learned about painting and books, but she discovered a side to Pedro de Zanto which warmed her heart as much as his physical presence thrilled her soul. With her he had no need to turn on his worldly charm. She was like a pristine notebook which he could fill with fascinating facts. She was to him, she felt sure, a youthful Galatea whom he was pleased to mould into a smoother creation than the rather gauche one he had first encountered.

After such an evening, wandering with him around his study, or seated on the great couch upholstered in Arabian saddle-leather dyed deep red as the skin of a pomegranate, Jaine would lie awake in her bed and relive every moment, every nuance of his voice, every fleeting smile. She was his pupil as Tristao was hers . . . it was only when she was alone, in the secrecy of her bed, that she turned a restless, seeking face into her pillow, and flung her empty arms across the spaces of her big, carved, canopied bed.

She had loved, and now she liked what she loved, and the two emotions combined were more exquisitely tormenting than anything in her life had ever been.

Came an evening when she paused to admire his beautiful marquetry desk, inlaid with exotic foliage and jungle creatures.

'So you are intrigued by our jungle?' He had poured old brandy into bell glasses and he handed one to her; it had been raining and the air was tangy, and a fire had been lit in the big tiled hearth. The flames cast shadows on the panelled shelves of books, and on the surface of the oil paintings. The Duque, clad in his dark-plum smoking jacket, took the huge armchair that matched the couch. He opened a jungle-wood box on the elbow-table beside his chair and took from it a cigar which crackled in his fingers and was bound to be of the best tobacco-leaf. 'Are the strange pagan rhythms of a jungle at night beginning to affect you, Jaine? You have a seeking and curious young mind, and having discovered freedom for yourself, you want a little more, eh?'

A flame flared upwards to meet the end of his cigar, lifting and falling as the rolled leaf took fire, revealing his features and then casting them back into shadow. When they had entered the study he had switched on the lights, which had faltered and died. Primitivo had come with candles in golden holders, and the Duque had explained to her that the power had failed, which it often did during a rainfall.

Jaine didn't mind the candles; she liked the romantic flicker of them, and the way they added to the atmosphere of this room, bringing into focus a topaz mask, the beauty and drama of a landscape, a mosaic bowl filled with black-purple orchids, and the brandy glasses engraved in diamond point.

'I have been thinking, *senhor*, that I should like to see a little of the jungle,' she admitted, curling down on the red couch with her honey-coloured skirt spreading out around her. Her hair was combed into short wings against her cheeks, and her eyes were dark as jade in the candle-light. 'One can't live close to it and not feel fascinated by it.'

'Very true,' he agreed, 'and I promise that you shall see it when I find the time to show you some of its interesting features, such as the beauty of a waterfall we call the Falling of Bitter Tears. But at present I am busy with regard to the new crop of coffee beans, and it may well be that I shall have to be away for a few days.'

As he said this, his brandy glass cupped in the palm of his hand and gently swirled to release the bouquet, Jaine cast a quick glance at his face and found it enigmatic and faintly mysterious in the flickering gold candlelight. She wondered if he would confide in her, her hope that he would edged by her reluctance to hear him speak of a woman; a Brazilian like himself, dark and vivid, her roots as deep in the lush land as the flame trees and the *copihue* that climbed gaily around the handsome trees.

Almost as if he read her thoughts he drawled quietly: 'There are plants in the jungle as alive as young animals, spicing the air with a thousand indescribable scents. Beauty and danger exist side by side, a tangle of silken flowers hiding the venomous *cascabel*, which is brightly mottled, fierce and quick. Or one may come upon a limpid pool, so enticing in the heat and yet likely to be infested with *piranha*, the cannibal fish whose sharp teeth can fillet a hand or a foot within seconds. There are few things more fascinating than an Indian fire-dance, but the entire performance is wholly pagan and erotic, for fire is a female element and the dance is to win her favour.'

The Duque slowly smiled through the fine blue curtain of his cigar smoke. 'I have never been able to decide which I find the more exciting, a fire-dance performed among the *papaya* and *chonta* trees, or the real gipsy flamenco performed in a smoky cellar. Have you ever seen a flamenco, Jaine?'

'Once in a film,' she said, 'but I don't imagine that was really authentic.'

'Hardly.' A smile of faint irony arched his lips. 'The true Latin flamenco is a duel between a man and a woman, not an exhibition for a cinema actress, stamping all over her partner's feet with a rose between her teeth. There is symbolism in the real flamenco, feeling and soul, and a passionate awareness that woman is huntress and man is hunter. Woman the sea; man the lightning. Woman the earth and the destiny; man the strength and the death.'

The Duque lounged in his great winged chair and his eyes were lidded, hawk-like as they dwelt upon Jaine.

'How young you are and how much there is for you to discover for the first time. Does the prospect not excite you, *menina*? Now that you are no longer duty-bound to that aunt of yours?'

'I work for you, *senhor*, so I owe you a certain amount of duty.' Jaine lowered her gaze and fingered the green sash of her dress. 'I am not a visitor in your home; I am here to work.'

'And are you liking your work?' he asked dryly. 'You have no regrets about leaving civilization for the wilds of Brazil? There are ample – compensations?'

'I still can't believe my luck,' she said ingenuously. 'I think I am one of those who are unhappy among crowds of people. I knew it but could do nothing about it – it is for you, *senhor*, to be satisfied with my work, for I find your *castilho en el aire* most beautiful and diverting.'

'My castle in the air,' he murmured, blowing smoke from his lips. 'Built strong and golden amid the acres of coffee trees, a fortress against the night and the enemy. It's a house which has been loved and hated by the women who have lived in it over the years, and it has out-lived their laughter and their tears. I have sometimes wondered if it is right or fair that golden stone should be more eternal than pale and passionate flesh. Have you an opinion upon that, Galatea?'

She was deeply startled that he should apply to her a name she had secretly called herself since he had taken it upon himself to become her tutor in the fine arts, refining the edges of her education, and adorning her person with fine silk and supple velvet.

'I – I always think the flower more touching than the vase, even if the vase is priceless,' she said. 'So it is with people, I suppose.'

'So it is with some people,' he amended. 'And I am not merely being cynical because I have lived longer than you, Jaine, and seen more of the world, but it is amazing how life itself is reflected by the jungle. There are the vines which strangle, the vines which adorn, and others which have to be searched out from their hiding places, and one has to take great care with these, for often when exposed to the sun they close in upon themselves, shrinking into their own petals and scent. They are often happier left in hiding, for unlike the exotics and the climbers they have an inward beauty rather than an outward one; they have deep hearts and they dread to expose them for fear of the pain that the more hardened jungle dwellers can inflict on them. They seek the shadows ... yet in the sunlight they can emerge as strangely attractive.'

As the Duque said this he rose from his chair and cigar in hand he walked to the red curtains and flicked them aside. He studied the rain that was again falling in a steady stream, making itself heard on the tiles of the patio outside the windows. 'I have to go away for a few days, Jaine.' He swung round and stood framed tall and dark by the long sweep of the curtains. 'I shall be leaving Tristao in your charge and I feel confident you will look after him well. You will not be nervous of being left at Goldenhawk among my Mayan people, with only the boy?'

'They're devoted to Tristao and getting used to me,' she said. 'I'll take good care of him, *senhor*.'

'I am grateful, Jaine.' He stood a moment studying the ash that was dark on the end of his cigar, then he re-crossed the study and laying the cigar in the groove of an ashtray on his desk, he opened a drawer of the desk and took from it a small black box. Jaine watched him, not really interested in

144

the box, her mind fixed upon where he might be going and with whom he might be staying during those few days of absence from Goldenhawk. Her gaze took in the ruby disc of his cuff-link and the lean strength of his hands in the candle-light. His hands, she thought, had the ruthless beauty of those to be seen in paintings by the old masters ... would they soon be touching another woman? Would they be as exciting to feel as they were to look at?

He moved from the desk and seemed to approach the windows again, and then she felt her pulses give a jolt as he approached silently behind her and she felt his fingers warm against her shoulder. 'Don't jump like that.' His lowered voice seemed to rasp in his throat. 'I am not a puma coming at you from out of the jungle.'

'Y-you walk like one, without sound.' She tried to speak lightly, but her heart felt so shaken ... she didn't want him to go away, but she had no right to want anything from Pedro de Zanto. She was merely his son's *confianca*, and here she was both thrilled and frightened by his light touch upon her shoulder. Then his hand moved and there was a soft weight and a warm glow in the pool of her throat, and his fingers deftly clasped the chain to which the object was attached.

Jaine glanced down wildly and there against her neck hung a carved green jewel; a deep and flawless green that was almost alive, with buried in the heart of it a stormy blazing fire.

'A dragon stone to keep dragons from your door,' he drawled. He circled the couch until he stood in front of her, then taking her by the hands he drew her to her feet and made her come into the candlelight. His eyes had a gold and piercing quality as they dwelt on the carved stone against the white skin of her neck. 'Yes, it is the colour of your eyes, and it almost seems to shimmer to find itself against the soft warm skin of a woman after so long hidden away in its black velvet bed. Well, Jaine, you seem a trifle stunned. What have I done, embarrassed your independent youth and shyness by giving you something when it isn't your birthday?'

'But – what is it?' She looked at him with wildly uncertain eyes. 'Is it valuable, *senhor*?'

'So-so,' he shrugged his shoulders. 'A minor dragon stone, pretty enough, but nothing that need give your virginal innocence a shock. I am not decking you in finery in order to excite my rakish impulses. I am feeling avuncular and I have noticed that you lack those gew-gaws so much delighted in by the female sex. Don't you care for the trinket, Jaine, when it seems to take such pleasure in being part of your person?'

'When I – I first came here, Tristao remarked that the Mayas call the emerald a dragon stone.' Her fingers were tense within the warm, lean clasp of the Duque's fingers; to him an emerald was only a stone because he had wealth, but to her it was a small fortune and weighted with all those decadent stories of girls who accepted such gifts from men. Her fingers began to fight for their release so that she might remove the pendant, and at once he sensed her intention and his hold upon her became impossible to break.

'It's an emerald,' she gasped. 'I can't – won't—'

'Ah, but you will!' His gaze dominated her, held her like a moth struggling on the shaft of a golden pin. 'I will tell you something – a man in my position finds few opportunities to express his thanks because he can usually afford to pay for whatever service is required by him. In the case of Tristao I could search high and low for the right person to care for him, at this particular time in his life. I am thanking you for placing yourself at the disposal of my son, not merely in the capacity of companion and teacher but as a friend, someone he can trust and turn to should anything – Miss Dare,' his hands gripped and shook her, 'we live in unsettled times, but a child must have someone close by who remains always calm, loving, and unafraid. These attributes you have, and I

146

require them for Tristao, and so to the devil with the possible worth of what I hang about your throat. It is an adornment, but if at any time you need money it is worth selling.'

Abruptly his grip was no longer that of a jailer, and quite purposely he drew her hands against the breast of his velvet jacket and held them there. 'Look upon the gem in that capacity, Jaine. I give it to you, for jewels are a currency in any part of the world, whereas a banknote can lose its value in a day. It is my way of compensating you should your stay in my country become suddenly – terminated. It is an assurance that you will not want, or have to return to some uncongenial occupation with people not congenial to you. Dare I say that you have found our company congenial?'

He held her gaze as he spoke, and though his eyes were serious, his lips weren't stern. Though his grip was firm, it wasn't painful any longer.

'No,' she murmured, 'it isn't uncongenial working for you, *senhor*.'

'I am right to assume that you have a fondness for Tristao?'

'Yes, *senhor*.' With a sort of inward desperation she schooled her face and her body, both of which could have betrayed how she felt about the Duque himself. 'I have grown fond of your son and I can only hope that my work here will continue for some time. I do understand that if you should marry I would not be required.'

'You think I have marriage on my mind – once again?' He looked at her with quizzical eyes. 'And who will be my bride, Jaine? Do you imagine I carry a still blazing torch for your seductive cousin?'

'I – I wouldn't know what sort of lasting effect a seductive woman has upon a man,' she replied, but in her heart Jaine sensed that whoever it was who called him away from Goldenhawk it was not her cousin. This call was more primitive, with the pagan rhythms of Brazil in it. Her cousin had been an interlude in his life; a golden toy for the amusement of Tristao at Goldenhawk – but a while ago, when Pedro had said that he was to be absent for a few days, there had been a smouldering flame of excitement in his eyes, as of a man who couldn't resist whoever – whatever called him away.

'I do assure you, Jaine,' he said dryly, 'that when I decide to marry I shall make a point of telling you about it. As you say, when that day arrives you will no longer be required as a *confianca* in my household. There, I am frank with you, for I know you prefer frankness to evasiveness.'

'I do, *senhor*,' she said, and her voice was more bravely steady than her feelings were. They felt painfully, tortuously shaken, and she knew that if the Duque didn't soon release her, her body itself would start to shake and he would guess that she was emotionally stirred up and he was the cause of it.

'You shouldn't really give me the emerald,' she made her voice sound polite and governess-like, 'but as I know you'll insist, being an obstinate man, I should like to go and look at it in the mirror. May I, please?'

'By all means, Jaine.' With a sort of amused mockery he slowly let go of her hands. 'When obstinacy deals with obstinacy there is always a bit of a battle, eh?'

'And the biggest always has to win.' Jaine walked to the door and opened it. There was a big scrolled wall-mirror in the hall and she could feel the tremor in her legs as she walked towards it, lit by candles in wall sconces of scrolled iron, so that as she became reflected in the mirror a kind of witchery seemed to cling around her figure, finding silky lights in her hair and stroking green shadows over her pale skin, facets of light flung out from the gem that clung and gleamed on a fine gold chain in the open neckline of the honey-coloured dress.

'Is that me?' Jaine wondered, and she had the oddest sensation of gazing upon a stranger there in the baroque mirror beneath the ceiling frescoes of deep smouldering colours. That was never Jaine Dare, but someone dressed in another woman's gown, wearing around her neck an emerald that like everything else was only borrowed. All of this was borrowed out of time, this love for a Duque, this romantic candlelight and the rustle of rain and brocade, and this elusive attraction lent to her by her rare surroundings and by a beautiful jewel she could never keep.

For several mystic moments she was reflected alone in the mirror, and then all at once she shared it with the imposing figure of the Duque. He towered head and shoulders behind her slimness, the plum-velvet of his jacket a dark rich frame for the snowy ruffles of his shirt, and a gleam of rubies at his cuffs.

'How slight you really are,' he said, and his eyes as they dwelt upon her mirrored eyes had something almost sombre in them. 'You have so much spirit, Jaine, that a man is inclined to forget how very unprotected you are by your youth and sensitivity. And yet – yet I would swear that I could depend upon you in a crisis better than anyone – it is only the flesh which is fragile, eh?'

'I like to think so, *senhor*,' she said quietly. 'You need never fear for Tristao while you are away from home. It wasn't out of cowardice that I stayed all that time with my aunt.'

'No,' he agreed, 'you felt it was your duty. Somewhere in your history there is a martyr and a fighter ... just look at this very straight spine.' He drew a finger very lightly down her backbone, and he wasn't to know that to Jaine it was like the touch of liquid fire from the nape of her neck to just below her waist.

'And somewhere along the line,' his teeth glimmered, 'a witch flew in and gave you a pair of bewitching eyes. Well, Jaine, what do you think of your pendant?'

'I should be very hard to please if I didn't like it, *senhor*.

It's kind of you to let me wear it—'

'*Madre de deus!*' His eyes glittered. 'Once and for all, I am not a kind man, *meninazinha*. Whatever I do, it is not done to be benevolent. I did not bring you to Goldenhawk because I was feeling charitable, nor did I give you the emerald because I was feeling sentimental.' His hands gripped her shoulders and he swung her to face him, and his glance as it went over her seemed to graze her like fire. 'Now don't be mock-modest or you will thoroughly annoy me. If a gem becomes a woman, then it should belong to her. Come, admit that you liked what you saw in that mirror, or I shall shake the truth out of you.'

'No, you aren't kind,' she said, and she tilted her chin at him and gave a slight smile. 'You have an artistic eye and even a humble *confiança* must be made to blend with all the lovely objects you have collected around you. You gave me dresses, but I had no jewel to wear with them, so you gave me a jewel. I thank you, *senhor*, but I can't pretend to myself that I have suddenly become beautiful.'

'Is that what you wish in your heart, that you were beautiful?' He stared down at her and it seemed to Jaine that the lift to his lip denoted his amusement.

'It is comical, isn't it?' she said. 'Like the clown wishing to play Hamlet, but I used to wonder, sometimes, what it felt like to be as pretty as my cousin. To have heads turn in the street. To have men in love with me, sending me flowers and chocolates, and taking me to first nights at the ballet. Yes, between the ages of sixteen and twenty I was hungry to know what it felt like to be as desirable as Laraine, and then at a party of my aunt's I heard a man make a remark about me which brought me very quickly to my senses. I don't dream silly dreams any more, and all I saw in that mirror was a plain young woman in masquerade, wearing a dress not hers, and a jewel that must eventually belong to your bride, or your son's when the time comes. I might accept a bit of green glass, but not an emerald, *senhor*. It belongs here at Goldenhawk. I'll wear it here, with pleasure, if you want that, but when I go away – well, *senhor,* there will be no more evenings such as these, no time, no place for emeralds. And as for selling it – that would be sacrilege! While a girl can type she can always earn a living.'

Jaine spoke bravely enough, as if she believed every word, but her heart sank like a stone at the thought of daily contact with a machine after knowing someone as alive and vital as Pedro de Zanto. Yet it had to be! It was inevitable! He had said himself that her time at Goldenhawk had a limit to it; that she would not be required indefinitely as *confianca* to the boy: as Galatea to the master.

Oh God, her heart so loved the strange and savage beauty of it all – the fiery flowers, the huge silky magnolias, the tropical singing birds that came to the patios each morning, where the ground beneath the jacaranda trees was matted with fallen petals from the beautiful mauve flowers, big as foxgloves. She could smell the tango vine and see the violet-eared, ruby-throated hummingbirds whirling in and out of that golden-orange vine they so loved. Petals and the aroma of coffee, and the Duque striding through the archway from the stables, clad in close white trousers and a tan shirt only a shade darker than his skin, in his hand a silver-shafted whip. Her entire being seemed to know him, so upright, so inimitable, the kind of person who came just once into a life like hers, with his fierce grace and pride.

Jaine saw the future as through a grey cloud, devoid of any magic, but she had to speak brightly of it, she had to pretend that when the time came to leave she wouldn't mind too much. She had learned that this man was kind in his own fashion and he might feel he had a duty to find her a place as companion in another household, but she wouldn't want to stay in Brazil if she had to live apart from him and Tristao. It would be better to leave altogether this land where the golden eagles fought in the skies, and where the golden-eyed puma roamed the jungle.

Despite the lightness of her voice, her eyes must have shown a shadow, for all at once the Duque took her chin in his hand and tilted her face to the sway and gleam of the candlelight. 'What is it?' he asked. 'Do you see a future without love in it? Do you fear there is never going to be a young man to turn his head, to give you flowers and sweets?'

'It won't matter,' she said. 'I've outgrown all that romantic foolishness, and I've accepted what has to be. It doesn't hurt so much once you accept what you lack — it's fighting it that hurts.'

'And what exactly is it that you lack?' In the shifting play of the candles his face was faintly satanic, and his left hand had slid down to grip her waist. 'Attraction is a strange thing, *menina*. Sometimes it exerts a pull upon a person quite against his will.'

'But I — I'm not attractive, *senhor*.' Her breath was coming quickly, half with fear of where this moment was leading, half with panic that he would sense her acute reaction to his physical closeness.

'And what has led you to this amazing and totally false assumption?' His voice dropped lower and he brought his dark, faintly taunting, pulse-quickening, dangerous face closer to hers, so that she seemed to be pulled into his tawny eyes, even as her body was pulled into his arms. It was all so tormentingly real, and yet so very unreal. She could feel the hard, masculine warmth of him, yet her own body felt boneless and weightless, as if composed only of nerves.

'It isn't false—' she shook her head. 'I overheard someone say — it was a man, that I had no appeal to — to men. I'm stuttering, being silly, and you're enjoying all this — tormenting me. It isn't fair, *senhor*. Don't look at me like that! I won't be mesmerized by you! You know your power over people—'

'But very transparently you don't know yours, *menina*. Who was this man, and what exactly did he say?'

152

'It was at a party, at my aunt's flat.'

'A theatrical party, eh?'

'Yes. Aunt Madge knows mainly theatre people.'

'And are you certain it was a *man* who made this remark about you?'

'Of course I'm sure it was a man.'

'You do understand me, Jaine? There are men, and there are the other sort – what exactly did this creature say about you?'

'He said – oh, can't you guess? He implied that I wasn't the type to appeal sexually to any man. A sort of pixie, born to sit upon a shelf, and to hop off every now and again in order to do the washing up and the clearing up, for my bit of bread and a sixpence.'

'So!' The Duque held her mesmerized despite herself. 'So that is it, some fop from out of the sexual shadows sees something unusual in you but cannot put a true name to it. Shall I, Jaine? Shall I tell you that you are a white-skinned young witch, with eyes of a very mysterious green? That you have an elusiveness that sets you apart from those candy-box young women who are really more passive than passionate? You may not know that the true flower of passion is a pale one.'

His smile was enigmatic as he ran a finger down the line of her cheekbone to the corner of her mouth. 'It was inevitable, little witch, that stones be flung at you.'

'Thank you for telling me.' Her only defence against him was to be pert. 'And now may I creep off to my incantations? I am rather tired, for I haven't yet grown used to your hot Brazilian days.'

'Tell me, will you regard this as a stone flung at you?' His fingers were at the emerald, so that she almost cried out as she felt his touch against the bare and sensitive skin of her neck. 'I warn you, Jaine, if you attempt to fling it back at me, there will be the devil to pay.'

'The devil in you, *senhor*?' She braved his eyes, whose

quizzical lights seemed to send quivers of feeling all through her, from her neck to the very heels of her feet.

'Yes, *meninazinha*, there is with a female a time to be subtle and a time to be savage, and though it suited me to be subtle when I suggested that you wear these very becoming gowns rather than let them hang in a closet, I am insisting that you accept the pendant.' His arm tightened painfully around her, and the indulgence was replaced in his eyes by a hard gold implacability. 'The emerald has nothing to do with the jewels which a Zanto bride would be given to wear. It is old – quite as old as this house – being one of the first gems mined out of Brazilian soil by the first Duque Pedro to live here. It was meant for the woman he never had the good fortune to marry, but it was given to her and used by the Wailing Doves to found an orphanage for Indian children, at which time it passed into the keeping of a rich Chilean, and it remained with him until a financial crisis caused him to sell it to a Russian countess. At the time of the revolution it finished up in France, where at the end of the Great War it became the property of a German baron. He took it home to his castle in Styria, where once again it remained for some years, until a sudden failure of the wine crop, when it was sold to a producer of wine in Portugal. As you know, Jaine, I was in Portugal a few months ago, and I saw the gem in this man's collection of *objets d'art* and I recognized it. I made a bid for it, but he would not sell. However, being a sporting man he challenged me to name the vintage years of six of his best wines – need I add that the jewel cost me quite a headache!'

'And after all that you want me to have it?' Perplexity and pleasure were all mixed up in Jaine, and then she quivered as a candle went out in a puff of smoke and a shadow seemed to fall over the Duque's face.

'It belongs to someone like you, for in the beginning it was mined and cut for someone like you. Innocent at heart, kind and sacrificing. I give it to you now, Jaine, because all is not right with this green-gold Eden of ours, and I may have to send you away quite suddenly. It is a good gem, and in its time has been used for good purposes. Keep it! It is yours!'

His tone of voice was explicit, his command was not to be argued with, and as he settled the gem in the pool of her neck he suddenly bent his head and kissed her on her startled mouth ... holding her lips with his until surprise gave way to a shafting sweetness in the very marrow of her bones.

She surrendered to his kiss knowing he kissed her because she was young, female, uncertain of her own appeal, and very much at the mercy of life, as lonely people are.

That she loved him, and felt the assault of that love, he didn't know, and wouldn't know. She held herself forcibly still in his arms ... while love like a velvet, tearing paw reached out and struck through her skin, to her bones, and her very heart.

She pulled free and blindly she turned away and through a blur of tears, snatching at her skirts with her hands, she fled across the hall to the stairs, and like a creature in a dream she ran without stumbling from the one person in all the world with whom she wanted to stay.

How hard it was to run ... how easy it would have been to fling her arms about his neck and be carried off alone with him, if only for an hour ... regardless of tomorrow ... regardless of that other girl he had put out of his life, the one who had given him Tristao.

She found her room as a hunted vixen finds its lair, and there in a smother of honey brocade she huddled on her bed, a hand clenched about the emerald which another *duque* in another time had given to a nun. In the strangest way it had acted like a talisman ... but it seemed such cold, hard comfort as Jaine crouched upon her great bed and heard the rain beating against the windows.

Her body still felt the impress of a pair of hard arms ... her lips still ached sweetly.

CHAPTER TEN

THE Duque left quite suddenly, without saying *au revoir* to Jaine. It was Tristao who told her that his father had come to his bedroom in the early hours and finding him awake had said that he had to go away – on business – for about a week.

'Papa asked me to be good, *senhorinha*, and not to cause you any torment.'

'As if you would, *amigo!*' She smiled, but inwardly she felt hurt, almost a stranger again, whom Pedro seemed to have forgotten on the eve of his departure. That interlude of the other evening might never have been, were it not for the emerald itself. She wore it continually, for fear of losing it; it lay beneath the collar of her blouse during the day, and by dusk fall the gem was so softly warm from contact with her skin that it had an almost magical lustre. Because Jaine had never been given very much she had been terribly unsure about keeping the pendant, but within a very short time it seemed to belong to her as nothing in her life ever had. It seemed to attach itself to her person, and during the few days before he left for his trip the Duque made no direct reference to it, only now and again did his tawny eyes rest upon the soft green glow of the gem.

With that innate courtesy, bred into the very bones of him, he made it possible for Jaine to accept the emerald, and she often thought how significant it was that like her love the gem was also green!

Goldenhawk felt strangely empty to Jaine after the Duque had left; she kept expecting to see him, strolling back from his early morning swim, or striding in from the direction of the stables after he had been riding the rounds of the coffee-tree acres. How the sun glinted on those miles of trees, with their glossy dark-green leaves and brilliant red berries. A single acre of good coffee-trees yielded a ton of beans. And then there was the plantation of silk-cotton trees, and upriver the fine forest of rosewood trees, whose oil was refined and used in the finest perfume.

It often occurred to Jaine that the Duque had a great deal of his capital tied up in the Goldenhawk estate, and because she knew that he was far from happy with the political situation in Brazil, she wondered during those long hot days what would eventually become of the lovely old place. He had admitted that nothing was permanent; he had said only the other evening that all was not well with their green-gold Eden.

Jaine glanced about her as she sat with Tristao on the veranda paved in coloured mosaics. Right now everything seemed heavenly (if she didn't allow herself to wonder who Pedro was with right this moment) and there was the boy, looking tanned and fit, feeding a woodpecker with a crest of bright red feathers. She smiled as the boy turned to her, his eyes like gold slanting leaves in his puckish face. Again she was struck by how like he was to that portrait of his young aunt, who was now far away in a Portuguese nunnery. Now and again he mentioned his Tia Maria, as he called her, and he often said how pretty she was in her big starched coif with the silver cross against her robe.

'I wish,' said Tristao, 'that we could go to the beach today. It's very hot, *senhorinha*, and we would be ever so cool down there.'

'Justus would have to carry you,' she said, tempted herself to plunge into that cool blue ocean, for when it was this hot the pool caught the sun and the water became tepid. 'I couldn't allow you to walk down, *amigo*, for if you had a fall and badly hurt yourself, your father would be fearfully angry with me.'

'Are you afraid of him?' Tristao limped over to her, too secure in the Duque's affection to have even a shadow of an idea of what it would be like to arouse his anger. 'But I have seen him smiling with you, Jaine. I think he quite likes you.'

'Yes, he quite likes me,' she said dryly, 'but he loves you, *caro*, and I daren't let anything happen to you. If I agree to go down to the beach, then you mustn't kick up a fuss if I ask Justus to carry you on his shoulders. He's a strong boy and sure-footed as a goat – I only wish he could carry me as well down that stony pathway.'

Tristao laughed gleefully at the picture, and grabbed a golden passion fruit as they made their way indoors in order to collect their bathing costumes and to inform Justus that he was required to act as porter for the *senhorito*. They walked along under the long-roofed, shady sweep of the veranda, past a massy curtain of mauve flower, and in through one of the latticed doorways, and Jaine thought how intensely deep must be the love of this place in someone who had been born here. Her fingers trailed over the carved cedarwood, which had the strength and sheen of chased silver, and a strange premonition took hold of her.

Something was in the air ... an intangible shadow that could not be seen but only felt. She drew Tristao to her side as they crossed the hall. 'Should we go?' she asked. 'While your father is away?'

'You promised, Jaine.' Tristao glanced up at her with reproachful eyes. 'I'm not a baby any more, and I want to grow up to be as brave as Papa. Primitivo says that Papa is one of the most valiant men in the whole of Brazil, and I have to live up to him. Besides, there are no waves in the pool, and I like being tossed up and down on the waves. The only thing I don't like is being carried – and when my leg gets stronger I will never, never be carried again!'

'All right,' she smiled, moved by the boyish plea, and the adoring wish that he be as much like his father as possible. Who could blame him for the hero-worship? She herself was equally captivated, and with little chance of ever seeing the boy grow into a lean young charmer, with a pair of wickedly seductive eyes. All she had was *now*, and that had to be made the most of.

'You go and find Justus,' she said. 'I'll fetch the suits and towels, and then I'll see if we can take a picnic to the beach. As it is such a warm day we might as well have our lunch down on the sands.'

'You are my *bom companheira* and I love you!' Tristao flung his arms about Jaine and hugged her with all his ardent, boyish strength. 'I love to eat the cold food on the ground, using just the fingers and not having to bother with knives and forks.Can we have cold eggs and drumsticks and olives and cheese—?'

'Yes, yes,' she laughed, hugging him in return. 'We will try and wheedle out of the chef all the nice things we like to eat, and today we will be a pair of beachcombers.'

He limped away eagerly in search of the Mayan boy, and Jaine felt a catch at her heart as she gazed after him. She must take great care of him, for the Duque was trusting her with the most precious of his possessions; the small human being who meant more to him than all the treasures of Goldenhawk.

About half an hour later they were on their way down to the beach, with Tristao comfortably settled on the strong shoulders of Justus, and Jaine carrying the suits, beach towels, and basket of food, to which the chef, a genial man, had added a flask of ice-cool pineapple juice.

As a sweet, wild wind blew off the sea towards Jaine and fluttered her hair and her skirt of dragon-red, she felt a stirring of pleasure made acute by a certain underlying ache. It was such a dazzling day; everything looked so blue-green and gorgeous, yet as Tristao's laughter floated to her, she felt the flawed perfection in it all. The Duque himself was far away, and because love had sharpened her instincts where he was concerned she felt quite certain that it wasn't a business affair that involved him. His plantations were too well run, his products too good to need his personal sales-manship. She had tasted the Goldenhawk coffee, wore at this moment a skirt made of the silk-cotton from the estate, and on her dressing-table there stood a flagon of the perfume to which the jacaranda oil had added its precious, subtle ingredient.

She paused on the pathway to the rockbound bay and watched the silvery swoop of the long smooth waves . . . they were as rhythmic as the beating of the heart, following an age-old design that never varied. And a'   them in the sky flew the sea-hawks with widespread wings, dark and graceful against the vivid blue.

Her heart, her mind, her vision, all were captivated by the tropical beauty that seemed so inviolable. She closed her eyes and took into herself this moment in time . . . whenever in the future, when this day was long over and she was no longer in Brazil, she would hold captive forever this blue bay overlooked by the house with the golden walls and the green gardens. She would hear the sea and the birds as they called, and forever on the wind the child of a man much loved would cry to her:

'Come along, *senhorinha*! We are leaving you behind.'

The words caught at her heart, for they seemed strangely prophetic. 'I'm coming, *amigo*,' she called in answer to the boy, making her voice seem merry and light. 'I'm just looking at everything, for it is so very beautiful today.'

'Girls are always daydreaming,' Tristao yelled. 'Run, Justus! Run the rest of the way!'

'No!' she cried. 'You will be careful with that boy, Justus! You will be very careful!'

Jaine hurried after the two boys and it was she who stumbled on the old worn steps and nearly tipped head-first to the beach, saving herself by clutching at a rope of liana growing out from the cliffside. The world dropped away at the side of the cliffs into the ocean itself, and Jaine felt a momentary horror that she had allowed Tristao to come down here.

Anyway, he and Justus were safely down on the sands of the beach, a sun-shot crescent enclosed in rocks almost the colour of red ochre, the ivory-coloured sands lapped by water as clear as an unflawed turquoise, its surface no doubt warmed by the hot sun but with cooler depths that would be like bathing in a deep goblet of Pernod over champagne. It was a drink which Jaine had never tasted herself, but she had seen her aunt drink it more than once, and that sea was exactly the same colour, with far out on the horizon a sheer jag of silver.

It was a secluded, rugged stretch of beach, and the air was filled with high-flung spray where the rocks were large and the sea gushed over them.

As she reached the sands she saw Tristao busily removing his sandals, and she was about to suggest that he ask Justus to stay with them, when the Indian boy slid past her, with his shy grin, and went running back up the steps to the headland.

'He could have stayed with us,' she said to Tristao, her gaze measuring the width of those long silver combers. She couldn't disappoint Tristao by not allowing him to go into the water, but she would have to insist that they took only a short dip and spent most of their time on the beach itself. She dare not let anything happen to him, for all she had of Pedro was his trust in her with regard to his son. If she broke that trust, her life itself would be a broken thing.

'Justus has no love of the sea,' Tristao was now busily pulling off his shirt. 'He much prefers the jungle, being a real Indian *patricio*, as I am Portuguese. It is in the Portuguese, *senhorinha*, to have a love of the sea. Papa says that the old captains of Portugal discovered much of the world, for they were very enterprising and adventurous. He says that is why we are friends with the British, for we have much in common.'

'Your father has a great love of Portugal, hasn't he,

amigo?' She helped the boy off with his shorts and assisted him into his bathing trunks.

'*Sim, senhorinha.*' Tristao smiled into her eyes. 'My grandmother was from there, and Papa has a sort of house at Estoril. It is castellated and it is where my *avozinha* lived, and it has a splendid park, with lovely waterfalls and little bridges humped over streams. And there is a dovecote paved all over with blue and gold *azulejos.*'

'It sounds like a castle,' Jaine smiled. 'And very pretty.'

'It is,' said Tristao earnestly. 'But in my heart I love Goldenhawk, for it is like no other house in the world, and the one at Estoril is like many others in Portugal. I want always to live at Goldenhawk, and when I grow up I shall ride about the plantations as Papa does, and go on puma hunts into the jungle, and attend the Indian councils. That is a very great honour – don't you think, *senhorinha*, that my papa is a very nice man?'

'Quite the nicest I have ever met,' she said, stroking the ruffled hair back off the boy's brow, and smiling into the gold-irised eyes. 'Now promise me you won't dare go into the water and will wait for me to change into my swimsuit. I shall be angry, Tristao, if you disobey me, for while your father's away you are in my complete charge, and I've given my word that I'll let no harm come to you. After all, you are all the family he has.'

'There is my *tia* at the convent,' Tristao gave a mischievous grin even as he reached out and touched Jaine on the cheek. 'They are brother and sister, you know.'

'I know that, imp, but your Aunt Maria isn't allowed any more to give her time and her affection to her immediate family. She is now a servant of the church and owes her first allegiance to the order to which she belongs. Your father can't enjoy her company any more, not in the way he used to. They can't go riding together, or enjoy concerts and parties together. You are his whole life, Tristao, and since your accident he is concerned that nothing so severe should

163

happen to you again. I believe, *amigo*, that he would strangle me if I allowed anything to happen to you while he's away. Now stay just here and play about with the sand while I change behind that big rock, the one that looks like a red knight with his head chopped off.'

'And who chopped it off?' Tristao wanted to know.

'Your papa, I shouldn't wonder, as he'll chop off mine if you get yourself drowned. You wouldn't want that to happen to me, would you?'

'No, because you have a nice smooth head like a blackbird's wing and your eyes have a sort of smile in them all the time, and I like the way you say things in your funny voice.' Tristao gazed at her with sudden solemnity. 'Will you be very old when I grow up, for I had thought about marrying you, Jaine.'

'That's very nice of you, Tristao, and I'm terribly flattered,' she said, with equal seriousness, 'but I shall be quite ancient by then, and you'll want a young and pretty girl for your wife.'

'How old are you now?' he asked.

'I'm twenty-two, *amigo*, and you can work out for yourself the great difference in our ages.'

He did his sums, but didn't seem too put off by the gap of sixteen years. 'I've never seen any other girl with eyes as pretty as yours,' he said. 'And I expect I shall look old for my age, with all the responsibilities I shall have. I shall be like papa, with those little lines in his face, that sort of get deeper when he smiles. Do you think I look like my papa, *senhorinha*?'

'Let me see,' she took his young face in her hands and studied the olive-skinned features that were more delicate than forceful. 'Yes, I see the family resemblance, Tristao. You have nice eyes yourself, just like your Aunt Maria's, but here in the point of your chin is the cleft that will get deeper as you grow older and then you will be very much like your father.'

'Your voice went all shaky when you said that – well, if you are frightened of my big father then I promise not to go in swimming until you are ready. But do hurry up!'

'Ready in a jiffy!' She ran behind the rock she had indicated and very quickly peeled off her clothes and stepped into her mink-brown, one-piece bathing suit. She didn't bother about a cap, for she had no expensive hair-do to spoil, and she smiled to herself as she recalled the elaborate rituals Madge and Laraine had indulged in when they went sunbathing. There were the protective lotions of the fair skin, a selection of a spot on the beach within sight and sound of male admirers, and the absolute necessity of being clad in the most stylish bathing suit. White sharkskin for Madge, and an eye-catching bikini for Laraine, neither of whom ever got wet, unless a muscular cavalier dripped sea-water over the luscious limbs.

Needless to say Jaine had cared more about the actual dip in the ocean, and as she ran to join Tristao she couldn't wait to feel the sting of the water on her bare legs.

In the water the boy was unhampered by his weak leg, but all the same Jaine kept very close to him and though had she been alone she would have swum further out and kept in the water longer, for it had an invigorating buoyancy that was like being bounced on champagne bubbles, she called a halt before he got tired and led a hunt for shells where the pale sand was pushed into small dunes around the rocks. Some of the shells were quite large and had a painted prettiness, and Jaine told the boy that if they found enough of them she would stick them all over a cigar-box – she felt sure the Duque would have one of those Romeo y Juliette boxes tossed carelessly into his wastepaper basket – and turn it into a memento; a shell-box that would always remind her of today.

Tristao handed her an orchid-pink shell with brown stripes, and his eyes asked a pensive question of her.

'Not yet, my darling.' She gently touched the tiny cleft in

165

his chin. 'But you have to realize that when your father decides to send me away I must go, for life is never just as we wish it. We have to store up the hours of happiness so that we can always look back and remember them on a rainy day, or when we aren't feeling too well. If we had too much joy, I think it might be too much to bear. We have to take the rough with the smooth; the sweet with the bitter, and that is what makes real people of us, able to endure the pain, and to distil every grain of pleasure, from the warm sands and the sea-shells, and the pineapple juice in our picnic basket. Shall we have some now? I'm awfully thirsty.'

'I – I don't want you to go away – not ever,' he muttered. 'When Papa returns from his trip I shall ask him never to send you away. If he married you—'

'Tristao!' The very words were strangely shocking, not because they came from a child, but they struck at the very heart of Jaine's hopeless dream. '*Duques* don't marry girls like me, *amigo*. I work for my living, and I haven't even the pretence of a pretty face. You mustn't ever say to your father what you have just said to me! Why, if you did that, then I should have to run away.'

'Why?' he asked obstinately. 'You are a girl, and men marry girls, and *I* think you are nice to look at. Your eyes are green like that jewel around your neck, and your feet are most pretty.'

'You, my lad, are the precocious son of a precocious father.' Jaine had to grin as she led him to where the picnic basket waited in the shade of a palm tree, leaning and whispering and casting spidery shadows. 'I appreciate your admiration of my feet, *amigo*, but grown-up men don't take wives on account of their toes being straight. It's usually the face they see first, and only small boys and puppy dogs like mine.'

He giggled when she said that. 'Oh, Jaine, you are funny!'

'That's just what I've been telling you, *mio*. I'm a sort of pixie, and I'd disappear in a puff of green smoke if you ever breathe a word of wanting me – of all people – for your father's wife. I'd make a glorious sort of *duquesa*, now wouldn't I? Can you picture me in a coronet?' She snatched up her straw sombrero and planted it squarely on top of her head. 'Her Excellency the Duchess Jaine, renowned for her straight toes and her straight hair, with a dash of the Irish blarney in her, which her relations take for sauce and her friends take for pepper.'

Jaine did a jig around the palm tree, playing the clown even as she longed to be a Juliet, possessed of a rare charm that so enchanted a man that even death was only a moment of hesitation before they were together again. Dream love, epic romance, and only to be found in books, which was both a consolation, and a bit of desolation which Jaine was too good an actress ever to reveal.

It was funny, but she had never given it a thought that she might have a bit of Madge's talent for acting in her bones, but all at once she had discovered her talent and was glad of it. She could always amuse Tristao, and always hide her true self from the Duque, and no one would ever know what joy, what torment, what fear of the lonely future lay in her heart.

'Shall we have our lunch now?' she asked Tristao, after they had quenched their thirst with a glass each of the delicious juice crushed from sweet, ripe pineapples. He nodded eagerly and they set to work on their picnic of cold wings of roast turkey, big tomatoes, hard-boiled eggs, juicy black olives, sliced sausage and meat patties. Tristao ate with appetite, sprawled out on the warm sands, with the sun on his legs.

'Did you used to have many picnics when you were in England?' he asked Jaine, biting into a shelled egg with a blissful look in his eyes. 'This is the nicest way in all the world to have lunch, I think.'

'It is good,' she agreed. 'I never went on a picnic as nice as this one before; my aunt always invited dozens of people, and they'd bring record-players and bottles of wine and make a lot of noise. A picnic is for being lazy and peaceful and *tête-à-tête* like we are.'

He nodded, and then said wistfully: 'I wish Papa were here with us. He would enjoy it, for he likes cold sausage and olives. I wonder what he is doing right now? Do you think he is very busy, and has forgotten all about us?'

'I'm sure he never forgets about you, *amigo*. You are always in his thoughts, for you belong to him as no one else in the world does. Mmmm, these meat patties are awfully good, with just the right amount of onion and pepper to flavour the meat.' Jaine smiled as she spoke, but she too was wondering, and wishing that Pedro was here . . . coming out of the sea with great drops of water on his brown shoulders, with that look about him of a flagrant, half-fearful masculinity, which none of the women in his life had ever tamed. Jaine closed her eyes and remembered the strength of his hands on the slenderness of her arms; the thrill of his touch that only her heart dared acknowledge.

The other night he had kissed her, but it had meant no more to him than a kiss he might bestow upon a niece or any young woman who happened to arouse his avuncular instincts. It wouldn't occur to him that a mere kiss could mean more to her than the jewel he had given her. He would probably smile and think her foolish if he knew that she treasured the memory of his lips far more than the Nun's Stone, which sometimes seemed to lay like a weight upon her breast.

'I think it would be great fun,' Tristao went on, 'to have lots of sisters and brothers, not only to play with, but one would never be lonely. Are you lonely, Jaine?'

'Not when I'm with you, *amigo*,' she handed him a fig which was so big and luscious it was almost transparent. 'You are eating a good lunch and will have grown another inch or so taller by the time your father comes home.'

'I hope he comes soon.' The boy nibbled his fig and his gaze travelled restlessly from Jaine to the sea, and she too watched the flurry of the spray and listened to the hiss of the waves as they slithered over the rocks. In the cliffside foliage the cicadas shrilled, and there where the trumpet flowers hung their bells the air swarmed with bees. Something was fretting the edge of her enjoyment, as it was fretting Tristao's. Disturbing the recesses of the heart as those bees flying in and out of the flowers, refusing to let them lie idle in the sun.

After his lunch the boy curled down upon the rug and fell asleep, but Jaine was restless and she wandered to the edge of the sands where the sea had grown quiet, and stood with her feet in the warm moist sand and felt the soft sea wind blowing her hair.

Yes, she too wanted Pedro to come home ... yet she couldn't shake off the feeling that when he returned things at Goldenhawk would never be the same again. Her gaze travelled to the sky as a hawk flashed darkly across her vision, and directly overhead there hung a single cloud against the speckless blue, and she gave a shiver as she looked at it, for it seemed strangely ominous as it hung there, and so symbolic of her thoughts.

As if to escape her thoughts she ran into the sea and struck out blindly through the blue shining water, and the moisture she blinked from her lashes had the sting of tears. She could almost have swum on and on until her heart stopped beating and the happiness had no finality ... no pain of severance from him who had made life come so alive for her. But his son lay sleeping on the beach and she must be there when the young eyes opened and looked for her ... and she was there and the sun had dried her hair when Tristao stirred awake and sleepily stretched out to touch her, as if to make sure of her.

'I thought you'd gone away,' he said sleepily.

'You've been dreaming, *mio*. I'm still here beside you,' she smiled.

He nodded and seemed content, but his fingers gripping hers had an intensity about them that was almost feverish, and she was rather glad when she saw Justus making his way down the cliff path, the big dog Arno bounding beside him. The reason for their arrival lay in the sky, for that single cloud had now gathered forces and it looked as if it might rain before the day was out . . . and Jaine already knew that when it rained in this part of the world it was like a curtain of swift-running water let down over the land. It beat flower-heads and palm-crests to the ground, and it blotted out the very sky. The tropical rain was as prolific as the tropical sun and foliage.

They returned home to the deep-walled, drowsy safety of Goldenhawk . . . strange how everything slumbered and seemed to hold its breath when the Duque was away. The heavily carved doors were closed against the red-gold clouds as dusk fell, but the rain held off as Jaine played dominoes with Tristao after their supper of crisply baked tortilla and tiny marrows with sweet potatoes.

At eight o'clock she saw that his eyes were heavy from his long day in the open air and he didn't have to be persuaded to undress for bed. She was tucking him in when suddenly he locked his arms about her neck and clung to her. 'You won't go away!'

'No, darling, I'll sit here until you fall fast asleep,' she assured him.

'I mean – ever?'

'Ever is a long, long time, *mio*, and right now I'm here and I'll only disappear in that green puff of smoke if you say anything silly to your father about me. I'm only your *confianca* and your friend, and to your father I am even less than that. I am his employee, and far less indispensable than Primitivo—'

'But don't you love me?' Tristao muttered against her, the

170

pressure of his young body pressing the emerald into her, so that even as she felt the pain she felt the joy of being loved and needed by Pedro's child ... the young male creature who was part of that big, dark, passionate man to whom convention was a snap of the fingers, but who couldn't indefinitely live unmarried and was almost certainly with a woman right now. The pain stabbed as Jaine imagined the Duque with the kind of woman he was born to admire, radiant and desirable, with eyes that met his boldly and didn't fall away in shyness when he looked at her; with the flair to respond to his ardour when he pressed his lips to hers.

'Of course I love you.' She pressed her lips to Tristao's temple, his cheek, and the side of his warm young neck. 'Now sleep tight, *chiquitito*, and have a nice dream.'

'What are you going to do?' he asked, his eyelids drooping as he gazed at her in the lamplight, the great dark pupils stealing the gold from his eyes.

'I am going to sort out all those pretty shells we collected, and tomorrow we'll find a box and decorate it.'

'Find it tonight,' he urged, 'so that we can start right away in the morning. Will you let me put the glue on the shells?'

'All right, if you'll promise not to get it all over yourself, so that the shells cling to you instead of the cigar-box.' She grinned down at him and stroked the dark hair from his forehead. 'That would be a shock for your father, to come home to a son made of sea-shells!'

Tristao grinned in return, and then snuggled down with her hand against his cheek. He was not a child to take a pet toy to bed with him; Jaine had discovered that this young Latin boy preferred living things to those that were inanimate, people and animals and plants. She studied him as he fell asleep, a child who was sensitive and responsive beyond his years, who had become attached to her because she was with him a great deal of the time. That, she realized, was why the Duque had thought of bringing a wife to

Goldenhawk in preference to a *confianca*. It was love of the child rather than love of the woman which had directed him, and as Jaine rose quietly from Tristao's bedside, easing her hand from beneath his cheek, she felt a rebellious, half-tender fury racing in her veins. It wouldn't matter about sending her away and breaking her heart when the time came. 'I do assure you, Jaine,' he said, 'that when I decide to marry I shall make a point of telling you about it.'

Her hand shook on the door handle as she let herself out of Tristao's room, and there on the gallery she took a deep breath as if to calm herself. 'I had to be insignificant,' she thought tormentedly. 'I had to fall in love with a significant man . . .' Her fingers clenched the wrought-iron balustrade as she made her way downstairs to the quiet, cool-tiled hall, where she paused in front of the wall mirror where the other night the Duque had stood reflected with her, so tall behind her, with eyes of an inscrutable gold by candlelight. Tonight she stood pale and alone and gone was the witchery which being with him had brought into being; the velvet dress seemed lank on her slim body, and the emerald seemed too foolishly exotic for a mere companion.

No, she didn't want to look at herself, seeing there a form and a face that could never excite to passion a man such as Pedro. She turned away from the mirror and walked to the door of his study, where she turned the handle and slipped like a ghost into the room which was always faintly redolent of Pedro's cigar smoke. She switched on the light and though the room was instantly filled with the colour and enchantment of the pictures on the panelled walls, for Jaine it was a lifeless room because the Duque wasn't there. The desk was too tidy, and the wine flagons and glasses glinted coldly on the side-table. Nothing was the same without the deep warmth of that Latin voice, with its slight accent and its many subtle shadings.

She sat down in the big chair of his desk and opened the lid of the century-old music-box of rosewood and mother-of-pearl. The old Portuguese tune tinkled gaily, while the pictures on the walls stared at her, almost insolent in their beauty.

Jaine knew that she tormented herself on purpose. That she came here deliberately to look at these rare and favoured *objets d'art* which the Duque had collected for his personal pleasure. 'Disharmony to the eye,' he had once said to her, 'is what discordancy is to music.'

He had an innate love of what was rare and lovely, and Jaine flinched from the self-inflicted pain as she touched the rosewood music-box, as she looked at the incised detail of the wine-glasses from which he drank, as she met the vivid eyes of a Dégas dancer and saw the swan-like grace of the pale slender limbs as the girl prepared for the ballet.

The lid of the music-box clicked shut and the music was stifled . . . Jaine rose blindly from the Duque's own chair and this time she fled unpursued from his study.

CHAPTER ELEVEN

THE days passed and the Duque's absence stretched beyond a week. No message arrived to explain why he was away so long, and though Jaine managed to convince Tristao that his father was delayed by his business contacts, she was certain in her own heart that it was something more deeply personal than the coffee trade which kept Pedro away from Goldenhawk for almost ten days.

The sense of unrest grew more persistent in her as the heat of the days seemed to increase ... a sort of recklessness took hold of her, and she told herself that if the Duque planned to return with a wife, then there would be no room at Goldenhawk for her. She was too young to be acceptable to any new bride of a man such as Pedro ... had he not said himself that circumstances could change and her stay could come to an end quite suddenly?

Friday dawned with a saffron-gold sun that filled the patios with a hot shining light patterned by the almost black shadows of the trees and benches. The tiny coloured birds who loved sweet things ignored the cake crumbs which Jaine and Tristao scattered for them and they hid themselves among the trees as if they found the sun too painfully bright. The dragonflies whirled in a mad vortex of purple and green, dashing filmy wings against the golden honeysuckle, and the cicadas shrilled persistently, unseen and unrelenting as the heat itself.

Tristao lolled about in his short green pants and his straw sombrero, while Jaine sought coolness in a chiton-type dress, sleeveless and flimsy. Her hair that was short, like those pages at the old Norman courts, didn't bother her, but as mid-morning approached she and Tristao went indoors, to the breezeway that ran right through the house from one end

174

to the other, providing an illusion of coolness on this the hottest day she had yet known at Goldenhawk. Arno lay sprawled out on the tiles of the floor, and through the arabesqued archways puffs of heat wafted in from the sun-drenched patios. The *cipres* trees hardly moved, standing there like spired ornaments of iron, and there was a metallic glint to the green curtain of creepers hung with immense lavender bells.

Jaine could feel the beating of her heart as she leaned against a tiled column ... deep apprehensive beats, like drums in her blood.

Being a Latin child Tristao rarely complained about the siesta habit and after Jaine had settled him down on his bed, naked as a brown imp under his netting, she went to her own room and attempted to rest on the *chaise-longue* in the deep alcove of her balcony.

'My chaste lounger,' she thought idly, tracing with a fingertip the enamelled flowers on her lemonade cup. In the cup was fresh lemon tea with mint and ice, and on the little lounge-side table was a plate of heart-shaped cakes stuffed with honey and nuts. She felt as spoiled and lazy as her cousin Laraine, and she wrinkled her nose in sudden displeasure and knew that her innermost urge was to get away by herself for an hour or two, where it was cool and secret and in tune with her restless mood.

She went out on to her balcony and stared down at the dense greenery leading off from the gardens of Goldenhawk. The jungle lay only a walk away and all that deep velvety green looked so cool and inviting, shut away from the brazen sun beating down on Jaine as she stood and felt the heat coming off the iron and tilework of her balcony.

'Are you scared?' a small voice seemed to whisper, taunting her as she stood there and felt the little beads of moisture on her upper lip and against the small of her back. 'Don't be silly, Jaine! The Duque is many miles away and surely pleasing himself in his leisure time.'

Jaine returned to her bedroom and picked up her shady straw hat on her way out of the room. She glanced in on Tristao to make sure he was still asleep, then ran lightly down the stairs in her sandals. The house was silent and she guessed that the Mayas had slung their hammocks and were also taking a siesta. She alone seemed bent on going out in the tropic sun, walking through the slumbrous silence and the patches of hot gold flung down by the sun, so relentless today that it had sapped all the scent and life from the flowers so that only the fiery poinsettia seemed vibrantly alive, the flame-like petals insolent in their gaudy beauty.

In the fruit groves the heavy pods of the banana trees hung motionless and the smell of cocoa was strong on the air. The little peaches called *paraguayos* gleamed among their leaves, and the skins of the avocados had a stretched sheen to them, as of fruits almost waxen in their richness.

A little further on and Jaine entered the jungle itself, with its mottling of green-gold shadows, great tangles of flowering liana, huge plumy ferns, and trees that gushed upwards like fountains, their leaves and branches laced together so that only glimpses of the blue sky could be seen.

Excitement caught at Jaine as she pushed aside the trailing lianas and wandered into this great lush nave, with its chorale of bird noises far up in the trees, its buzzing of insects, and chirring of cicadas. In here they were not stunned by the sun and they created around Jaine a living wall of unseen life, never silent and never still, so that she was less nervous than if she had found the jungle a silent place. She gazed with wonder at the towering flamboyants that seemed aflame in their own flowers. She saw bushes weighted with sheaves of mauve blossom, and trees wrapped in vivid, diaphanous scarves of pink and yellow vine. It had a strange glamour, this wild green Eden which Pedro had known from a very young child. It had a wild beauty and power which would appeal to him, and there would not be a plant not known to him, nor a sound to which he couldn't put a name. He would have an affinity with this place, for despite his title and his culture there was a pagan streak in the Duque; something as unchained, as ruthlessly strong and graceful as the jungle trees.

Then in the fork of a tree Jaine caught sight of an orchid similar to the one the Duque had given her, her first day at Goldenhawk. She reached for it and plucked it lightly from its nook, purple-brown speckled with the sheerest gold, and so remindful of what Pedro had said about the aliveness of jungle plants and flowers.

Jaine marvelled at the elegant design of the wild orchid, which would look exotic and lovely tucked into the raven hair of a Brazilian woman . . . someone like Felicia de Evangel who at one time had nursed the Duque's sister during an illness, and who had seemed on very warm terms with the Duque. Jaine hated the trend of her thoughts . . . hated this side to love, that made her see him so vividly in the arms of other women. It was such a one-sided torture, for she meant nothing to him and was hurting herself in vain, like some martyr walking with open eyes into a hedge of thorns.

It wasn't until she had wandered a little further into this strange wilderness, both forbidding and fascinating, that Jaine realized that she was wandering in a jungle where it would be all too easy to become confused. Its beauty was deceptive and she knew there was danger here, in hiding among the colourful creepers, lulled by the murmurous hum of the insects and the twitterings of the small birds flying high in careless rapture. She thought of those jaguar skins that adorned the floors at Goldenhawk, some of them tawny and velvety, others with a patterning of black rosettes on the pelt of deep yellow.

As she looked about her she felt a faint tickling on her arm and discovered that a praying mantis had settled lightly on her skin, its gauzy wings fluttering and then folding in the absolute stillness of its praying attitude. It was pale green and so delicately made that Jaine felt it was hardly believable that such a pretty, luminous thing should be so innately cruel ... there had been one clinging to a lamp-shade in the study one evening and the Duque had told her, with a faintly cynical smile about his lips, that the mantis probably prayed for absolution, for it was in the habit of killing its lover.

'Fly away, you deadly beauty,' she whispered, and the tiny slanting eyes in the strange triangle of a face seemed to look at her, then the wings fluttered open and it was gone, disappearing upwards into the trees. Jaine followed its flight, and it was then that she noticed how gloomy it had grown above in the high canopy of interlaced branches, and as she listened she caught the patter of rain on the big leaves, and her skin quivered as penny-sized drops of water began to fall upon her bare arms and neck.

Heavens, she had better hurry back before she got drowned! She began to run, feeling all the time the quickening plip-plop of the raindrops, and aware of the humidity as of a giant greenhouse in which the plants began to give off a wildly primitive scent, a mixture of leaves and loam incredibly rich and greedy for the rain. The jungle darkened as clouds rolled over the sun and blotted it out, and then suddenly it was lit again by a streak of silver light, flashing on the boles of the trees and etching leaf and flower in vivid detail.

Alarm took hold of Jaine ... here she was among thousands of trees and and a tropic storm was about to unleash itself. What a noodle she was! She might well have guessed that a day so hot could only lead to this ... and she flinched as another whiplash of lightning flickered down through the trees and curled around her fleeting figure. And to top all the rain began to hurtle down, and her dress of thin material began to cling to her like muslin.

She ran as a maddened mouse-deer might run, heedless of

everything but getting out into the open, where the crash of the thunder was preferable to the forked danger of the lightning among the trees. The vivid flashes were relentless and violent now, lighting her way out of the jungle which had grown almost black and filled with the drowning noise of the tropical downpour. Lances of lurid light and blackest shadow crossed like foils across her path, and bushes and branches she had earlier avoided were now reaching out to hinder her and to scratch at her arms and legs.

'Oh ... God!' She had run violently into something and thought it a tree until her wild hands gripped a body with the strength and flexibility that could belong to no other human being in the world but the Duque himself ... except that that was impossible, for he was miles away and she was running mad in a forest of natural furies.

'You might well call upon the Deity!' Voice, hands, words came from out of the nightmare turned to an impossible dream. '*El Diabo* himself might well have answered you, but it is I ... do you hear me, you foolish, half-drowned ... Jaine, stop trembling like that or you will dislocate every bone of your body!'

'*Senhor* ... Pedro ... is it you? Her fingers dug into him, and in the white shock of the lightning she saw his face bent to hers, the tawny eyes glinting ominously, the features a mask of rain-wet, golden fury. It was he, balm in Gilead, or hell itself, she just didn't care which it was so long as she felt him, saw him, and was so gripped that she was bruised and awake in the storm that pounded and drenched the two of them. Never, never had she seen him look so angry ... he looked as if he might kill her, except that he suddenly bent lower to her and thrusting her back against a tree his mouth descended fiercely, with ferocity and a terrible kind of sweetness.

'Small, crazy, absurd Jaine.' His hand was stroking over her wet hair, from which the straw hat had been struck by a flying branch. Warm, insistent down over her neck and her body, to which the dress was attached like a piece of wet rag. The slanting rain struck at them, and the sky seemed to ripple with white fire. She felt the hard warmth of his body through the thin silk of his shirt, for he had opened his jacket and dragged her inside in an attempt to shield her, and as she clung to him, she seemed drunk on the jungle scents, lost with him in some impossible heaven.

'It's dangerous . . . here under the trees,' she said, and her voice was all shaken to pieces by the pounding of her heart.

'It's dangerous . . . anywhere,' he said. '*Por deus*, the flimsy things you women wear! And you talk of danger!'

'I mean the lightning,' she buried her face against him as the fangs of sharp silver edged with blue snapped around them like a puma hungry for the kill. 'Pedro, let's make a bolt for it . . . please!'

'In a moment, *carestia*, when you get your breath.' His fingers were lean and caressing against the nape of her neck. 'In any case I think you are more afraid of me than you are of the storm, which is all quick furious temper which will pass in a while. What is between us can never pass, now can it?'

'I – I don't know what you mean,' she mumbled, for honestly speaking she didn't know what occasioned this show of fierce tenderness and temper all mixed together. The only facts she could analyse in her present state of confusion were that he had arrived home and had come looking for her; that they had blundered upon each other . . . and had kissed.

'Stop being evasive,' his fingers gripped her chin and held her face away from his chest, forcing her to look up at him. 'You don't get kissed as I have just kissed you, Jaine, for being a strayed *confianca*. You get that kind of punishment, and I hope pleasure, for being a white little witch who steals my heart with her emerald eyes, and who touches me with thin young hands and sets my blood afire. Heaven and hell, Jaine, if I've been wrong and you don't love me—?'

'Love you?' she said dazedly. 'I've wished I didn't – I've tried not to care – you – me? We're poles apart!'

'I would say, Jaine, that we are but two skins apart,' he softly, mockingly contradicted her.

'Y-you are talking about bodies, I am talking about position—'

'Really, *alma captiva*, this conversation becomes more provocative by the minute. Our position strikes me as being a very enticing one, even with the rain pelting down and the lightning playing its fire in and out of those bewitching eyes of yours.'

'You're deliberately twisting my words,' she twisted a little against him, as if to escape, and at once he locked her so closely to him that it was an actual pain to feel his muscles pressing into her. '*Senhor*, please, this is madness, and when the storm is past you'll wish you had never spoken to me in such a way.'

'You mean, my child, that I shall thank the storm for making it easy for me to speak this way.' He gazed down at her pale wet face, filled with the dark green glimmer of her eyes. 'It is the strangest thing that a man finds it so much more difficult to make love to the woman he adores than to the passing flame which he very soon extinguishes. I sometimes thought that in the tranquillity of my study I might speak of what lay in my heart, but somehow the moment never arrived – that perfect and exact moment. It had to come *now*, a storm within a storm, eh?'

'I – I am your son's companion,' she said, opposing him even as she longed to submit, to give in, to believe even against all the odds. 'I am poor, not much to look at, and very insignificant. I don't know what it is that you want of me, but I – even with you – I won't cheapen what I feel by having an affair with you. There! I've said it! It sounds awful, but I mean every word!'

'I am sure you do, you strange, unworldly creature you.' He spoke the words against her temple, his breath playing warm and fast against her skin. 'Ah, Jaine, you'd fight for honour even in my arms, wouldn't you, and my arms are your home and your heaven, if you will only believe me. I love you, my child. Your simplicity has a whirlpool at the heart of it, and I am lost in it. I see integrity and courage and witchery when I look at you. I see the woman I want. The woman I shall have, if my pilot manages to get that plane off the ground in a tropical storm. Come, it is time to run – time to go!'

'But I don't understand—' Her eyes pleaded with him. 'What do you mean about the plane? Where are we going?'

'With luck, my darling heart, to Portugal.' He swept the plastered hair away from her eyes and bending his tall head he kissed her wet face, his lips travelling all over her features, warm and rain-tasting, and loving. Jaine could feel the loving, and her heart felt as if it might choke her.

'Pedro – please!'

'Don't you like me to do this? My heart, you will have to get used to it, for I mean to do a great deal of kissing to make up for all the lack of it.'

'Pedro, you're driving me crazy.' She pushed her face into his hard shoulder in an attempt to escape his lips. 'I want to know what's going on! Where have you been? I thought you were with – with someone—'

'A woman?' he mocked. 'Come, this is no place for explanations, and there is not much time left to us. It was good of the storm to come, for it will keep away those who are eager to get to Goldenhawk before I do what has to be done. Hold fast to my hand, *carestia*, and run with me all the way home!'

For the rest of her days Jaine would remember the remainder of that night, the strangest she ever lived through. When they reached the house, Primitivo was in the hall with warm ponchos into which they were wrapped right away, and there was hot coffee and brandy. Tristao was dressed and wrapped against the rain, and bits and pieces of baggage had been hastily packed. The jeep was standing in the forecourt, and as the Duque hurried them out to it, the rain began to ease off and the thunder had passed. It had surely passed, and yet Jaine could hear a throbbing from the direction of the jungle, and Tristao's finger tightened around hers.

'Drums,' he said excitedly. 'Papa, the Indians are saying *adeus* to us.'

'Yes, my son.' Pedro lifted the boy into the jeep, and by the courtyard lanterns Jaine saw that his face was firm and set, like a savagely beautiful mask.

'In with you, my dear.' He was roughly tender with Jaine as he settled her in her seat. 'Primitivo will run you to the plane, which is waiting on the runway, and then he will return for Justus and myself. They are coming with us ... they are not being left behind to fall into the hands of those who are turning my country into a place of fear and oppression. With a woman?' His laughter rang out, the diablerie of it mingling with the sound of the drums. 'My dear, I have been whisking certain friends out of the country with the help of Felicia de Evangel's husband. We got her on to the boat this morning and they are well on their way to Portugal. Now off with you, Jaine, and please don't look back. Just go to the plane and wait there with Tristao. All will be all right. Trust me!'

The jeep started up and made for the archway that led to the driveway. Jaine did glance back and saw Pedro striding back into the house.

'Primitivo,' she cried out, 'what is he going to do?'

'He is going to set light to Goldenhawk, *senhorinha*. He is going to burn his house and the plantations.'

183

'Oh no!' Jaine crouched in her seat and closed her eyes with the pain of it. 'Must he do such a thing? Is there no other way?'

'Not for him, *senhorinha*.' A soft note of pride rang in the Mayan's voice. 'It is the land and heritage of the Zantos, and it is for the Duque de Zanto to put Goldenhawk to the torch rather than have it fall into the hands of bad men. The Senhor Duque is a great, fine, brave man, *senhorinha*. He will not be forgotten in Brazil. He has risked his life to save people from being tortured by the military. Indeed, he will be a man remembered, and a man with a price on his head every second that he remains in Brazil, but the burning has to be done. There has to be time for that.'

Goldenhawk, she thought tormentedly, her arm locked around Tristao as the jeep sped through the darkness to where the private plane awaited them. So this was how it must end, all that beauty and grace and history put to the flames . . . so this was how it must begin, a man, a girl and a child in flight from the green-gold Eden, with joy and hope of finding another.

Just over an hour later when the plane took off into the night, the darkness and the jungle were lit by the flames of Goldenhawk, burning amidst its coffee acres, its cotton trees and rosewood oil, a great red-gold pyre of flames, above which the plane circled in a last farewell.

Fighting the tears in her eyes, Jaine glanced at Pedro as he peered with her from the window beside her seat. His face in that moment had almost a cruel sadness as he reached for her hand and held it tightly to the edge of pain. 'Goldenhawk was ours,' he said. 'Goldenhawk will be ours for always, for no one shall have it who has no claim of loyalty or love. No one again shall walk in its gardens, take coffee beneath the magnolia trees, nor listen to the voices of the jungle on warm still nights. What was Goldenhawk will be our memory, intact, unravished, gone to its glory in the clean gold flames.'

And when he spoke like that Jaine's tears could not be held back and very slowly they rolled down her cheeks.

'Don't cry,' he murmured. ' "The best is yet to be." '

The plane flew on through the night, and when Tristao's young head drooped tiredly against Jaine, the Duque lifted him and carried him to a couch where he soon fell asleep, the lashes dark against the young cheeks.

'He is so like his dear mother.' Pedro lightly touched his cheek, and seemed unaware of the tortured look which Jaine flung at him.

Dear mother! Dear father in heaven! She turned away and stared blindly from a window into the night spattered with stars.

'Jaine?' His hands were suddenly upon her shoulders, possessive and warm. 'Please listen, and after I have explained, we'll speak no more of the matter.'

'His mother – you love her still?' Jaine couldn't look at him; could not endure to see a similar look to the one that had been upon his face when he leaned over the boy.

'I shall always love her, my darling.' His head bent to hers and his lips just touched her earlobe. 'She is my sister Magdalena. Her fiancé died, a child was to be born, and I did what it was best to do. The boy became mine and Magdalena took the veil. I wished it otherwise, for I hoped she would love again, and marry, but she wanted the father of her child and no one else. Then I did not understand – but now I do, with every atom of my frame, every nerve of my body, every beat of my heart. I know what it is to adore one person beyond all others.'

He turned Jaine to him as he spoke, and Jaine couldn't speak for the strangling sweetness of the moment. The Duque Pedro de Zanto looked deeply into the eyes she raised to him, and then he carried her hand to his lips and as she felt them, warm and lingering, there shot through her a flame of such intolerable joy it was almost beyond bearing. No more words were needed ... their eyes spoke and their hearts knew that somehow, somewhere, they would build anew their Goldenhawk ... together.

THE OMNIBUS
Has Arrived!

A GREAT NEW IDEA
From HARLEQUIN

Sara Seale

Omnibus

Her natural talent for creating the very finest in romantic fiction has been acknowledged and enjoyed by a great many readers since very early in Miss Seale's career. Here, we have chosen three perfect examples of her best loved and most cherished stories.

. . . . CONTAINING:

QUEEN OF HEARTS . . . when Selina presented herself to her new employer at Barn Close, the exclusive country hotel in Coney Combe, Devonshire, Max Savant had one thought, to send this "child" on her way. Now, it was impossible for him to imagine himself, or his hotel being without her. But, he must, for he has just become engaged to Val Proctor . . . (#1324).

PENNY PLAIN . . . at Plovers Farm, near the village of Chode, in England, Miss Emma Clay is employed as assistant and companion to the rather spoilt young lady, Mariam Mills. Their relationship proves to be rather stormy, not the least cause of which is the country vet, in his country tweeds, the uncompromising Max Grainger . . . (#1197).

GREEN GIRL . . . Harriet listened to the incredible suggestion that she marry this total stranger and thus solve her dilemma, and the trouble which he himself was in. Whilst she knew full well that her own plight was quite hopeless, instinct warned her that Duff Lonnegan's trouble was far more serious than even he knew . . . (#1045).

$1.75 per volume

Jane Arbor
Omnibus

Jane Arbor chooses inspiring locations, peopled with the most life-like characters, — then inter weaves her gripping narratives. Her achievements have brought her world renown as a distinguished author of romantic fiction.

. . . . CONTAINING:

A GIRL NAMED SMITH . . . Mary Smith, a most uninspiring name, a mouselike personality and a decidedly unglamorous appearance. That was how Mary saw herself. If this description had fitted, it would have been a great pleasure to the scheming Leonie Crispin, and could have avoided a great deal of misunderstanding between Mary, Leonie and the handsomely attractive Clive Derwent . . . (#1000).

KINGFISHER TIDE . . . Rose Drake was about to realize her most cherished dream — to return to the small village of Maurinaire, France. To manage her aunt's boutique shop produced grand illusions for Rose, but from the very day of her arrival, they were turned to dismay. The man responsible was the town's chief landowner and seigneur, a tyrant — living back in the days of feudalism . . . (#950).

THE CYPRESS GARDEN . . . at the Villa Fontana in the Albano Hills in Italy, the young, pretty Alessandra Rhode is subjected to a cruel deception which creates enormous complications in her life. The two handsome brothers who participate come to pay dearly for their deceit — particularly, the one who falls in love . . . (#1336).

$1.75 per volume

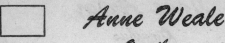

Anne Weale

Omnibus

The magic which is produced from the pen of this famous writer is quite unique. Her style of narrative and the authenticity of her stories afford her readers unlimited pleasure in each of her very fine novels.

. . . . CONTAINING:

THE SEA WAIF . . . it couldn't be, could it? Sara Winchester the beautiful and talented singer stood motionless gazing at the painting in the gallery window. As she tried to focus through her tears, her thoughts went racing back to her sixteenth birthday, almost six years ago, and the first time she set eyes on the sleek black-hulled sloop "Sea Wolf", and its owner, Jonathon "Joe" Logan . . . (#1123).

THE FEAST OF SARA . . . as Joceline read and re-read the almost desperate letter just received from cousin Camilla in France, pleading with Joceline to come and be with her, she sensed that something was terribly wrong. Immediately, she prepares to leave for France, filled with misgivings; afraid of learning the reason for her cousin's frantic plea . . . (#1007).

DOCTOR IN MALAYA . . . Andrea Fleming desperately wanted to accompany the film crew on the expedition, but Doctor James Ferguson adamantly refused stating that if she went along, he would refuse to guide them. But, Guy Ramsey had other ideas, and cunningly devised a scheme whereby Andrea would join them — in a manner which the Doctor could not oppose . . . (#914).

$1.75 per volume

Essie Summers ②

Omnibus

Without doubt, Miss Summers has become the first lady among those who write of the joy and splendour of romance. Her frequent use of locations in New Zealand, the country of her birth, has a timeless appeal to her readers throughout the world.

. . . . CONTAINING:

HIS SERENE MISS SMITH . . . she was very certain that never again, under any circumstances would she ever become involved with a member of the male management of any firm where she was employed. Then, William Durbridge came thundering into her life, and before long, was making his way straight to her heart . . . (#1093).

THE MASTER OF TAWHAI . . . Tawhai Hills Estate lay deep in the green rolling country of South Canterbury, New Zealand. It was here that the wealthy young Rowena Fotheringham came to work in the hope of being accepted for herself — not her fortune. She could easily have been, had she not decided to deceive the very first man who had ever really cared for her, complicating both their lives . . . (#910).

A PLACE CALLED PARADISE . . . no one must ever know the truth, the reason why Annabel Lee had come to Paradise, an isolated plateau at the head of Lake Wakatipu in New Zealand. She did not know how deeply she would come to love a man called Gideon Darroch, nor how it would affect him — if he learned her secret . . . (#1156).

$1.75 per volume